SEP 2010

The Mourning Wars

The
Mourning Wars

KAREN STEINMETZ

ROARING BROOK PRESS | NEW YORK

For Donald, Andrew, and Kate

Text copyright © 2010 by Karen Steinmetz
Published by Roaring Brook Press
Roaring Brook Press is a division of Holtzbrinck Publishing Holdings
Limited Partnership
175 Fifth Avenue, New York, New York 10010
www.roaringbrookpress.com

Distributed in Canada by H. B. Fenn and Company Ltd.

Library of Congress Cataloging-in-Publication Data

Steinmetz, Karen.
The mourning wars / Karen Steinmetz. — 1st ed.
p. cm.
Summary: In 1704, Mohawk Indians attack the frontier village of
Deerfield, Massachusetts, kidnapping over 100 residents, including
seven-year-old Eunice Williams. Based on a true story.
Includes bibliographical references (p.).
ISBN 978-1-59643-290-1
[1. Indian captivities—Fiction.   2. Mohawk Indians—Fiction.   3. Indians
of North America—Fiction.   4. United States—History—Queen Anne's
War, 1702–1713—Fiction.]   I. Title.
PZ7.S8276Mo 2010
[Fic]—dc22

2010011735

Roaring Brook Press books are available for special promotions and premiums.
For details contact: Director of Special Markets, Holtzbrinck Publishers.

First Edition August 2010
Book design by Natalie Zanecchia
Printed in the United States of America

1 3 5 7 9 8 6 4 2

PART I

EUNICE WILLIAMS OF DEERFIELD
OCTOBER 1703–APRIL 1704

CHAPTER 1

"Don't forget, Mary!" Eunice Williams calls over her shoulder to her friend as they leave their lessons in the meetinghouse, "Tomorrow you are to show me the stitch you are working on."

"I'll bring my cloth to school," calls Mary, turning toward her own house outside the gate in the stockade at the south end of the village of Deerfield. "And tomorrow we'll have more time. I'll be living inside the stockade near you!" Eunice lives in the brown clapboard house across the street from the meetinghouse, where her father, the Reverend, preaches every day and twice on Sundays.

Indian summer has crept over the frontier town after a solid week of cold rains. Glad to be sprung from the schoolroom, Eunice is dazzled by the sun, the world all mud and spangled brilliance. She lifts her loose-hanging sleeves and flaps them like a bird to create some movement in the still air. Her six-year-old brother John copies her, throwing back his head and raising the hem of his long baby clothes. Her brother Stephen, who at ten dresses like a man in loose shirt and pants, stands apart from them regarding his siblings' game with a look of disdain. But as they round the back of the meetinghouse, all three throw back their heads, spread their arms, and turn in circles as they drink in the blue and gold of the autumn sky.

"There must be a breeze by the river." Eunice slows down, bringing the world back into balance. "We might find cress growing there." She looks at Stephen expectantly. Though at seven she is closer in age to John, she considers Stephen to be her closest companion.

"Oh, do let's beg a whipping from our father!" snorts Stephen in response. "You know he'd punish us if we were to be caught outside the stockade." Eunice frowns. For two years now, ever since the beginning of Queen Anne's War against the French and Indians in Canada, her father has been worried about attacks. Eunice can barely remember what it was like to go down to the river with Parthena and Frank, her family's two slaves, but she thinks often of how cool it was in midsummer, damp, pungent, shady, with cress growing in the shallows like food for some mysterious otherworld creature.

Now, despite the late autumn heat, Reverend Williams won't allow his children to go down to the river with anyone. There have been reports that English towns on the Maine and Vermont borders have been raided by French soldiers and their fiercest Indian allies, known as the Maqua. The men of Deerfield have been working hard, not only to get in the last of the hay but also to mend rotten places in the stockade, where the tall wooden pickets have loosened, and build temporary shanties, barely houses at all, for families like Mary's who must move inside for protection.

"I'd rather go and see how our fort has held up in the rains," Stephen declares, walking around their house toward the weathered stockade at the back of the yard. Eunice runs to catch up. Before leaving for school in Boston, their eldest brother Eleazer showed them a sketch of a lean-to he'd seen on an earlier trip. Local Indians had built it, he said, or maybe voyaguers, the French adventurers who live like Indians. After studying the sketch, Stephen and Eunice collected sticks and hemp sacking and managed to erect a fairly sturdy structure against a section of stockade at the back of their yard.

Eunice had found it good fun playing Indians, until their father began preaching about the heathen hordes in the north that would come sweeping down upon the sinful inhabitants of Deerfield. The people of Esau, he called the enemy. "Let my people go," he prayed. Trying not to squirm on the hard seat during her father's long Sunday sermons, Eunice began to worry about their game; it is hard to know when one is sinful. So before the rains began, she had convinced Stephen that they should be voyageurs, trading in Albany with both the English and the Dutch, and owing allegiance to no one.

But now Stephen won't let Eunice be a voyageur and keeps insisting on calling her a squaw. "Why should I be a savage when you won't anymore?" she complains. "'Tis not fair play when you keep calling me that." There is something sickening about being an Indian woman among the French, though Eunice can't tell why.

"You can't be a man, Eunice. 'Tain't true to life at all. And only savage women travel with the Frenchmen."

"I won't play if I must be that." Eunice bites her lip and glares.

"Then we won't play." Stephen shrugs. "You can't be a voyageur, Eunice. 'Tain't right, is it?" he asks, turning to John, who trails behind them ignoring their bickering. John nods, but Eunice doesn't think he minds what role she takes.

As they pass the north parlor window, Parthena calls out, "Miss Eunice, come get your baby brother. He wants to go with you."

"We're going to look at our fort," shouts Stephen. "I guess Warham can come."

Parthena gives four-year-old Warham a pat, sending him running toward Eunice.

Heading down the incline a quarter mile beyond their house, Stephen lets out a whoop. "It stands!" he shouts. "Pretty woodsmen we are!"

But their lean-to looks smaller than Eunice remembered. They lift a sacking cloth to get inside. Eunice has to pull Warham onto her lap to make room for the four of them, and even then they can hardly move without nearly bringing the whole structure down. They have built the lean-to against a part of the stockade where a loose picket can be pushed aside disclosing a sliver of the hayfield, neatly mowed and running down toward the river. Now, Eunice pushes it so far that even Stephen can squeeze through.

"Why don't you try it?" urges Eunice. A strand of damp hair curls into one of her eyes, and the stiff stays in her dress, meant to keep her back straight, poke her just below the ribs when she bends. As she leans into the opening, a slight breeze makes her face go prickly. Barn swallows skim the stubble left by haying scythes. "Just for a minute. The hay is all stacked now. No one will know. I'll go if you won't."

Stephen slides feet first through the opening into the hazy light of the late afternoon. Eunice cautions her two younger brothers to wait and pushes through head first behind Stephen. Her long overskirt gives her some trouble, and her red cotton gown catches at the waist as she pulls herself through.

She feels the seam give way. "Fie!"

On the other side of the stockade she inspects the damage and straightens her skirts. The river glimmers beyond the tree break. She might fix the tear before anyone notices. The mud on her over-skirt will be more troublesome. But the breeze is delicious. Eunice and Stephen sit for a few minutes, their backs against the outside of the stockade, saying nothing until they hear John begging to join them.

So, into the mowed hayfield crawl John and Warham. Stephen has a small deerskin ball dyed red and yellow and stuffed with calico scraps, which he begins tossing in the air. He shoots it un-expectedly at John calling, "You're the Savage!"

The game continues until Warham misses, and the ball rolls down the slope toward the hayfield, giving Stephen the opportu-nity to go a little farther into the field. Stephen and Eunice begin to miss the ball on purpose, laughing as they fumble and then scram-ble to get it.

"That first haystack is not very far," Eunice darts a look at Ste-phen. "If you run to it, I'll follow as soon as you've tagged and climbed it."

Stephen looks doubtful. "If we're caught 'twill be the devil. And who do you think will pay dearest?"

"We're scarcely outside. I can't think anyone would fault us for it. 'Twill only take a moment to get to the haystack and back." Eunice gives him a little prod.

"All right, we'll do it. Just us two, though." He warns. "'Tis growing late. There's only time for two of us to go."

"You and Warham go back and be lookouts in the yard," Eu-nice tells John. But John insists on staying and if he will not leave, Warham must stay too.

As Stephen takes off, Eunice watches with her heart in her

mouth. Danger is part of the game: if they are caught they will surely pay with a beating. She herself has had only one whipping, once when she was little and she set out for Mary Brooks's house without permission. Since then, she has had no more than a cane across her hand for foolishness. The joy of being out in the open field beyond the stockade after being shut inside for weeks makes the risk worthwhile.

Far ahead Stephen gains the haystack, but then he just stands looking off toward the river.

"Why doesn't he move?" Eunice mutters under her breath. "Climb it!"

John pulls at her sleeve. "Someone will see him!" He pipes.

"Hush!" says Eunice, finger to her lips. "He'll do it."

And he does, waving from the haystack, a slender figure haloed by the sun. "My turn now. Don't dare to follow me," Eunice whispers to John. "And keep Warham with you. You're both too little to climb it."

Stephen slides down from the haystack while Eunice unties her unwieldy overshoes, kicks off her thin-soled slippers, and takes off. The thrill of fear that courses through her evaporates as she slaps hands with Stephen passing on his way back the stockade. Hair streaming behind her, scalp prickling, Eunice is aware of nothing but the sweet smell of hay, the slippery wet stubble under her stockinged feet, and the wide golden sky suffused with lavender, orange, and crimson. She doesn't even hear the commotion behind her, doesn't stop until she reaches the haystack and turns to see Parthena's husband, Frank, racing toward her, nostrils flaring like her father's bull's. Mahogany forehead furrowed with a furious intent, Frank sweeps her into his arms and turns back toward the stockade at a fast trot. He is breathing too heavily to speak until they have safely reached the stockade where only Stephen waits now, having pushed the younger boys in through the gap when he saw Frank coming.

"You're a lucky miss that your brother came along, Miss Eunice." Frank has put her down and is leaning heavily against the stockade. "It be the devil to pay when the Reverend hears about this, and I'll be telling him too, miss. He has to know. And your little brothers followin' you! What were you thinking of? Wanting to be made a savage? A devil Maqua mayhap? Now get you back inside. I be mending this hole when I come round."

Eunice is amazed at the anger in Frank's voice. This gentle man has never so much as spoken sharply to her before. As Eunice pushes her way back through the gap, she is weeping with fear, not of Indians, but of her father. She is sure of a whipping this time.

Frank puts his hand on Stephen's shoulder, "Master Stephen, your father'll be proud of you, getting your little brothers in from the field."

Eunice, listening from within the lean-to, is sobbing too hard to shout that it was Stephen's idea too, that the Stebbins and Hoyt boys are allowed in the field and even go nutting in the hills sometimes, and that no one has seen any of these fierce Maqua or Frenchmen from the north.

Stephen is quiet for a few minutes, and Eunice crouches, seething at the injustice until she hears him tell Frank that he too has been playing in the hayfield. She is amazed, for he will surely get a beating.

• • •

"Go and tell Frank to tear down that devilish lean-to and patch up the loose picket where the children got through," her father commands Parthena as soon as he hears about their game. Her father's face is dead white now and his mouth is a tight seam that barely opens to let the words out. His eyes light on Eunice only briefly.

"Eunice, get you upstairs with the little ones," he tells her. Then he looks to her eldest sister Esther, just returning from the Carter's with their mother. "Esther, see that she waits upstairs. I'll attend to her next," he commands. "Stephen, you well know I cannot have my own children playing games outside the stockade when I've ordered the whole settlement in. Come." Eunice watches from the landing as her father takes a cane from beside the back door and leads Stephen outside. Her mother moves to say something but shuts her mouth and turns away.

CHAPTER 2

He therefore that went before (Vain-confidence by name), not seeing
the way before him, fell into a deep Pit, which was on purpose there
made by the Prince of those grounds to catch vain-glorious fools
withall; and was dashed in pieces with his fall.

—The Pilgrim's Progress, *John Bunyan*

In the morning, Eunice sits copying the lesson her father has set
for her. The letters of her book squirm, and she aches for Stephen, alone upstairs with his smarting wounds. They have been
forbidden to see each other or to leave the house. Her lesson from
The Pilgrim's Progress is all about a man named Christian, who must
carry a heavy burden through terrible trials and temptations before
he can reach Beulah Land and enter God's Celestial City. Writing
has always given Eunice trouble. It is easier for her to do it in
stitches where the colorful patterns make more sense. The Reverend will surely not think her copy fair. Her fingers, so quick to do
her bidding with a needle, are clumsy with a quill. Her mind keeps
wandering up the stairs to Stephen, and the ink seems to dry before
she thinks to dip the pen. She wants to tell Stephen that she would
never in a million years have given him away. At least she thinks
she wouldn't. Eunice still cannot think that what they did was so
very evil. Again she feels the exhilaration of her race through the
stubbly field, feels her hand slap firmly against Stephen's in sweet
solidarity.

Parthena is slicing apples to be dried for the winter. The room is dizzyingly fragrant with the sweetness of them. But Parthena will neither look nor smile at Eunice.

Eunice looks closely at her mother, who is settling the folds in her cloak over her growing stomach before heading out on her errands. She notes the weariness beneath her mother's calm. What was it Eunice heard Goodwife Carter say to Parthena last summer? Her mother had been out, and Parthena had whispered something under her breath to Goodwife Carter.

"Not following so hard upon the last one?" came Goody Carter's reply. Then lower, "I wot not how the Reverend could be so careless! A body needs time to rest after losing a child."

Eunice thinks of the twin sisters who lived so briefly the winter before, but she still doesn't understand Goody Carter's complaint. Her father has always seemed a careful man to her. Now she looks at her mother's pale face, framed by a blue and white bonnet and a few escaping strands of reddish hair, and wonders what Parthena and the Carter woman meant.

"Parthena, look to it that Eunice improves her time with her lesson. I would not have her idling or telling tales while the others are in school. The Reverend Williams is greatly wroth with her." Eunice's mother speaks sharply as she makes ready to leave and avoids looking in her direction, causing Eunice as much hurt as the cane across her palm where the welt between her left thumb and forefinger still smarts.

Eunice notices that Parthena looks stricken by the reference to her tales. Despite mild disapproval, her parents have been tolerant of Parthena's storytelling. Once, when her mother tendered some concern, Eunice was surprised to see her father look up from the sermon he worked on, catching her mother's eye with a conspiratorial gleam in his own. "A bit of spice from the Indies will not hurt the children, as long as they are taught to sift true from false. And Parthena is as good a Christian as any of us." It was a secret look, one quick to disappear. When he returned to his sermon, her father's face reclaimed its stern rapture. But ever after, Eunice has smelled nutmeg and cinnamon in Parthena's stories.

She looks up to the window from her copying to catch her mother's blue cloak receding along the road as she leaves the Stebbins's house, Esther beside her. Her mother is forever carrying on the business of her father's parish. She often takes Esther along, leaving Eunice with Parthena on the days when she is not in school. But she is usually sure to tell Eunice about her visits for the day. Eunice looks longingly at her mother's back, wondering where she is heading. She wishes she could go with her instead of copying lessons, smelling apples, and not daring in her disgrace to beg a slice.

Outside the kitchen there is a simmering vat of pokeberry for crimson dye. Despite the steam rising from it, Eunice wants to go out and stir the purplish-looking mixture, and dip a rag to see if it will take the color. Better still, she wishes she were at school with Mary Brooks. Mary will be looking for me, thinks Eunice. And she knows she will not be allowed to eat dinner with the Brooks family when they come tonight, and she will have to wait to learn Mary's new stitch. Eunice whispers the words under her breath instead of copying her lesson, "Now, Christian and his fellow heard him fall. So they called to know the matter, but there was none to answer, only they heard a groaning. Then said Hopeful, Where are we now? Then was his fellow silent."

Wiping one palm on her orange calico apron, Parthena holds some apple slices cradled in her other, "Don't think badly of the Reverend," she says comfortingly, seeking Eunice's eyes. "He had a bad scare. And don't you worry about Master Stephen. His pride is hurt more than his back is."

Eunice knows this is not strictly true.

"You scared my Frank half out of his wits," Parthena continues. "And the Reverend had a worse scare before that. He might should have told you children about it. There's some think it was just a panther he heard, but he was near captured himself the other night, when he went looking for stray cows by Broughton's hill."

Eunice looks up in surprise. "He never told us," she says with some doubt. "How do you know of it?"

"He told your mother that he saw two men creeping like savages in the bushes. He had to leave off looking and come galloping home. Why, my Frank, he didn't even want to go out to the field hisself yesterday for fear of those devils. And then he sees you and your brothers running through the hayfield!" There is a hint of scorn in Parthena's voice.

Eunice looks thoughtfully at her, trying to assess the truth of what she says. Parthena has never told tales about the family. But why would her father not tell them if he saw savages creeping in the bushes?

"He might should've told us," she replies sourly, echoing Parthena's manner.

CHAPTER 3

It turns out there is more that her father hasn't told. Eunice hears it the next day, when Joanna Kellogg, one of the older girls, whispers something to Stephen as they approach the meeting-house for their lesson.

"No!" Stephen exclaims in amazement.

"'Tis true. All they found was Zebediah Carter's hat with two bullet holes in it and some blood." Joanna is too worked up now to whisper. "My brother Joseph says the savages left the hat on purpose, as a message. That's how they know that Zebediah and John Nims are truly captives."

Eunice looks to Joanna in wonder. The attacks in Maine have seemed distant. But this is like the story of the Belding family being carried to Canada years ago when Eunice was a baby. Eunice looks with a shiver toward the northern gate, where her fifteen-year-old brother Samuel will be working all day. She thinks of Zebediah's wife, Sarah, how pretty she looked coming out of the meetinghouse after her wedding last summer.

"How do you know they weren't killed?" she asks Joanna.

"My brother Joseph says they would have found the bodies. The Maqua know people will bargain to get the captives back."

This seems likely to Eunice, and it gives some hope too. After all, the Belding family came back and lived in their house just outside the north gate until they moved inside the stockade a few days ago. But what will they bargain with? What is it the savages want?

. . .

That night high winds sweep in, carrying cold rains. Eunice's father does not wait until Sunday for the church service. Because of the news about Zebediah Carter and John Nims, he has called a day of fasting and praying in the meetinghouse. And he has sent a messenger to Boston asking for some additional soldiers to keep watch. Sitting on the hard bench in the meetinghouse, Eunice thinks her father's sermons have taken on something of the dark thrill of Parthena's hant stories from the Indies. Lately, he always asks that God spare his people from the heathen scourge and smite the enemy in his tracks. Today, Eunice is so hungry that she can hardly follow her father's words.

"We ask the Lord to deliver us from the evil hand of Esau's people. But when He may release us, we know not. Therefore, we must search our hearts for the evil within and accept as our due the affliction sent by a righteous God." Her father's voice rings out over the congregation, angry and regretful, as if he is disappointed that his people have caused the terrible punishment that has arrived, as if there will be more to come. Eunice remembers being very small and mistaking his voice for the fearsome voice of God. It frightened her even more to realize that it was her father speaking.

Eunice does not like to think of such an angry God, or to think of having heathen enemies all around. Then again, the stockade looks very high, and the Indians she has seen on occasion here in Deerfield do not seem very savage to her. And didn't Mary Caitlin marry a Frenchman? But when Eunice starts to wonder about these things, weighing them against the disappearance of John and Zebediah, she is silenced by the thunder in her father's voice as he looks out over his congregation and asks them to search their hearts for the sins that have brought God's wrath upon them. Is not all misfortune a measure of God's righteous anger, a sign that they may be damned for all eternity?

The bench seems especially hard today, and Eunice's right foot has fallen asleep. She slides down so her foot can reach the floor to work the prickling out, but Esther gives her a stern look. Stephen sits on the other side of the meetinghouse with Samuel and the men. She can't see him without moving. Being in the front row, the Williams family must set an example, and her father notices if she fidgets. He will ask later what kind of devil she's let in. Sometimes he seems to be teasing, but she isn't sure. The day goes on forever, it seems, divided between sermons and silent prayer. Her hunger gnaws at her. The fast will go on until tomorrow morning.

$$\bullet \quad \bullet \quad \bullet$$

The days grow shorter, and the snow comes early and heavy. As winter settles in, Eunice's father seems to her to have grown sterner and more on edge. When he requested more militia from Boston, only a few men arrived, and he does not seem to trust them. The smallest errors set him off, and Eunice must try very hard to be good. Some nights they have neighbors sleeping in the side parlor because the roofs of their shanties have collapsed under the weight of the snow. They crowd in with Frank, Parthena, and Eunice's youngest siblings, John, Warham, and the new baby their mother gave birth to just before the snow came, a baby girl named Jerusha. Eunice sometimes lies awake at night listening to the talk and the baby's frail cry and thinking of the infant twins who died the previous winter. Esther sleeps deeply beside her. Tonight there is only her own family in the house. The chimney is not drawing well and the house is smoky. She can hear her parents talking before they get into their bed in the main parlor.

"I heard it again last night. It didn't sound like wolves to me," says her father. "It was high-pitched, but it didn't have that mournful sound. There was excitement in it, something more devilish than any sound the wolves make." Eunice can picture her father pinching the narrow bridge of his nose and squinting at the embers in the fireplace, the way he does when he's worried.

"I can't think what it could be but wolves," her mother answers calmly. "The militiamen have been out to scout and saw no signs of footprints or any other disturbance."

"The snow has been falling so steadily that a person in those snowshoes the savages fashion might leave no mark by morning. I am not a fearful man or I would never have come to this post, but I cannot explain what I have heard these past two nights. You know I am not alone in marking it strange." He pauses. "I have never felt my responsibility weigh heavier. I do not trust the guard they have sent us from Boston. They are too few, and I suspect they are idle men. More interested in eyeing my elder daughter than in the signs the townspeople have seen and heard."

"They might well look at Esther. She has grown into a young woman," her mother replies. Eunice can hear her settling herself.

"She is a child, nevertheless," retorts the Reverend. "I am going upstairs to check on the children."

"Surely they are fine."

Eunice listens to the creak of her father's footsteps as he comes up the stairs. He looks first into the older boys' room to the north side of the staircase and then crosses to the girls' room. Here the pale light of a waxing moon throws patches of light from tiny crescent-shaped windows. Eunice closes her eyes, pretending to be asleep, afraid he might scold her if he finds her awake. He stands for a moment over the bed, then leans over and strokes her cheek, uttering a prayer before he turns away.

CHAPTER 4

Can it be morning? Eunice's mother is quietly crooning her name while rocking her gently from sleep. But despite the crooning and rocking, her fingers dig painfully into Eunice's shoulder, surprising her into consciousness. Opening her eyes, she can barely make out her mother's shape in the dark. Eunice can see her breath making wispy ghosts in the winter chill of the upstairs bedroom, and she can feel that the bed is empty and cold where her sister should be sleeping beside her. As her mother's voice dies away, beyond the deadly quiet of the room, there is a commotion that Eunice's sleepy mind cannot sort out. There are shots. The baby is crying downstairs. She hears John cry out. Parthena's voice rises above the others. But she no longer hears them.

"Eunice, you must wake up!" Her mother is whispering urgently in her ear. Her grip remains tight, but its firmness is soothing now. "Be still, my girl, and do as I say. Our lives depend upon it. You must not make a sound but only listen. We are to be taken captive."

Eunice begins to protest, but her mother continues to hold her tight, rocking her all the time.

"Shhh! Shhh! I have your clothes. I will help you dress now. There is a savage in this very room. He will not hurt you if you are meek. Pray God that we may keep together. We must dress you."

Already her mother has raised Eunice's arms up. Awkwardly helping her to find the sleeves, she pulls the heavy dress over her head. For a moment, like an animal in a trap, Eunice feels a sudden panic of comprehension and struggles against her mother. When her head emerges from the muffling clothes, the room remains pitch dark. No candle has been lit. Calmer now, she peers into the darkness trying to locate the savage, but she can make out only a shadowy form that must be Esther.

"Esther! Help Eunice with her shoes. You mustn't move or make a sound unless I tell you," her mother cautions. There is a hoarseness in her whispering voice that Eunice has never heard before.

Eunice is surprised at the sureness with which Esther slips on her overshoes and ties them over her instep in the darkness. Even so, the tying seems a small eternity. All that she hears now comes from outside. There are shouts and gunshots and an uncanny ululation, weird as the high-pitched chortling of wild turkeys in the spring. Where is her father? And Samuel? She can make out Stephen nearby now, for there is a flickering of light. But the light comes not from within the room but from outside, as if from a bonfire. Eunice registers half consciously that the blaze is from the shanty the Hawks family built on the corner of the lot when they moved inside the stockade.

The door to the hall is opened, and a man is shoved through it. It is her father, followed by two men dressed in skins, their painted faces gleaming in the flickering light of a burning brand. One of them has Warham by the arm. Eunice wants to scream, but her mother wraps her arms around her, pulling her face into her chest to silence her as she whispers "Hush!" to her older sister and brother.

Her father's voice sounds choked, each word wrenched singly from him as he addresses her mother. "God has seen fit to take our John and the baby. Parthena too. She would not let go the children. We must bear ourselves meekly if we are to be preserved."

There is no more than a stifled sob from her mother, a small whining sound in her throat, which lasts only a second before Warham is delivered into her arms.

What does he mean about John and Parthena and the baby? The room is very still. For the first time the shuddering light reveals the stranger in the corner. His head is shaved, all but in the center, where it stands up stiffly like a brush, and his lean face is halved by blue and black paint. Over his shoulder he has draped the blue wool and calico quilt that yesterday lay stretched on her mother's quilting frame. At his feet she sees that her brother Samuel lies bound on the floor with his arms behind his back.

It seems to Eunice that they sit in silence on the bed forever, listening to the shots and the strange cries that transform their town into a weird, ungodly place. They are all shivering in the cold though they wear as many clothes and blankets as they could find in the dark. As the sky through the little wedge-shaped windowpane begins to turn gray, several more savages file into the room carrying guns. Surely they will all be killed together now. Eunice presses her face into her mother's shoulder.

Instead there is low, unintelligible talk among the men. Then they are ushered down the stairs. As she comes to the bottom Eunice looks for Parthena and John and the baby, but sees no one. Are they killed or only taken away? Who will bury them and give the sermon? Her father's and Samuel's hands are still bound behind their backs as they step out into the snow, and Eunice can see that it is difficult for them to keep their balance as they walk.

They find themselves joining a nightmarish procession herded by the French soldiers, some in bright uniforms and helmets, and the painted Indians, all of them stumbling ahead in the new snow. When the snow first came down so heavily in January, her mother said that God had sent a blanket to swaddle them. But it has not protected them from the savages and now just makes it very hard to walk.

Shots continue to ring out from somewhere behind them, and the smell of damp fires is everywhere. In front of the Carters' house, Eunice sees blood in the snow and a green homespun coat that looks like Mr. Brooks's. She pauses to look, but her mother suddenly drops her hand and encircles her in her blue cloak as she pulls her forward. Stumbling to keep up, Eunice tells herself that it is not Mr. Brooks by the road. It is a stranger in his coat.

The deep snow drifting up against the tall stockade has allowed their enemies to scale the walls but has prevented them from opening the gates much more than the width of an angel's wing. One by one the captives are urged stumbling toward the empty white world beyond.

It is impossible for the smaller children to walk on their own beyond where the snow has been cleared. The line slows as people stop to lift children onto their backs. Eunice lets go of her mother's hand as her father, wrists unbound by one of the savages, lifts her onto his back and tells her mother to be brave and stay close to them. As they move away from the burning town, those who are walking wade thigh deep in snow, causing their captors to prod and push them to go faster. Occasionally, those least able to keep up are dragged off into the trees. The others are forced to keep moving.

As they get beyond the drifting snow, an icy glaze under the new powder makes it possible to walk on top of the snow without sinking. The Reverend drives his heels into the crust to keep his footing. Eunice, clinging to his back, sees in the pale dawn that Samuel is carrying Warham not far ahead of them. Stephen and Esther walk ahead on their own, unimpeded, urged on with a group of older children. Eunice cannot look behind her without unbalancing her father even more.

"Mother is not with us! Let us wait for her," Eunice implores.

Her father's voice, strained and weary, comes out in gasping breaths, "Our masters will not allow it, child. We must let the Lord protect her. God willing, she'll be with us soon. Look ahead now."

When they reach the river, there are dark patches on the ice, thin places where the water still runs swiftly. How cold the water must be! Eunice looks ahead to the treacherous ice. She sees a man's leg go through ahead of them, and the other leg start going, until he seats himself abruptly and one of the savages pulls him out. Eunice forgets and tries to twist her head around to look for her mother again, but her father staggers as her weight shifts. She knows they risk breaking through one of the thin places if she doesn't keep still so her father can step carefully.

When they reach the far side of the river, the tree trunks look slick and black in the pearly light and reflect the rose hue of the rising sun. Eunice is terrified when her father continues to stumble. Each time he loses his footing she expects to be taken from him by the savages that flank them. Her poor father. She knows she is too heavy for him in this snow, but she knows too that she might not get very far on her own. She is afraid to whimper or cry out and looks longingly ahead to where she can make out Stephen and Esther.

"I can walk," she insists.

"Hush!" Her father gasps with such vehemence that she is silenced.

Eunice's eyes are drawn back to the two Indians who seem to have special charge of them. They seem like figures from a dream. And perhaps she has dreamed them during the weeks when so many neighbors crowded inside the stockade, and stories spread like smoke from a clearing fire. Descriptions of the fierce Maqua wafted from house to house, coming in at the windows and down the chimneys in the night just as the Maqua themselves seem to have come. Now Eunice finds herself unsurprised by their appearance. In fact, the shaved heads and painted faces look familiar to her, terrifying but expected, like a lightning storm come down from the mountains. It is hard not to look upon their captors with the awe of recognition. So this is what we have feared!

Between captives and Indians, they seem to be a whole army setting off for the north. Or, thinks Eunice, it is as if the whole town had set off for a sugaring party, for they are heading in the direction of the Stebbins's maple grove, and Eunice has had sugaring on her mind for weeks, knowing that the sap will be running soon. As the company wends its way through the maples, it is hard not to imagine the foaming vats of sap, the heat and the smoke and the ribbons of maple syrup hardening in sharp, sweet designs in the snow. She can't imagine that she will not be in Deerfield for sugaring.

"How long till maple sugaring?" she asks her father, as she has asked so many times in the past few weeks.

"'Tis a frivolous thought, Eunice, with our homes burned and so many dead behind us," he replies sharply.

There are at least as many Indians and French soldiers as colonists among them, and the going does not seem much easier for them. Ahead of them a tall man with feathers hanging down one side of his head supports another, half carrying and half dragging him through the snow. Eunice notices that there is blood on the twigs and leaves in the tracks that her father steps into to keep his footing. But beyond a blank registering of sight and incident there is little thought of anything but the necessity to keep moving.

As the straggling band comes together beyond the river, Eunice's father, flanked by two Indian masters, is allowed to bring his people together for a prayer and in doing so is able to assemble what remains of their family. All but Eunice's mother. Eunice doggedly drives a stick through the crust of snow until she looks up to see the folds of a blue cape beside her. She rises so swiftly to embrace her mother that one foot breaks through and she looses her balance and falls, scraping the back of her leg on the jagged ice. Her mother gently disengages her leg from its icy trap.

Sweeping her into an awkward embrace and looking intently into her eyes, she says softly, "We must thank the Lord that we are reunited for a time. You must remember, Eunice, that even when we are parted I go with you. And the Lord will watch over you too, if you be brave and obedient."

Releasing Eunice, her mother looks lost for a moment. Then coming to herself, she fumbles for a moment beneath her heavy cloak, withdrawing a small silver cup. "Try to keep this, Eunice. But 'twill be a small matter, if you can't," she says. She tears a blue cord from her cloak and ties it around the cup's handle, fastening it beneath the apron of Eunice's dress.

Her father recites the Lord's Prayer and then preaches of the Israelites being led into Egypt in bondage. Eunice looks questioningly at Stephen, who shakes his head at her. They mustn't speak while their father is praying, but Eunice is filled with wonder. Could they be taken into Egypt?

When the prayers are finished, Stephen turns to Eunice. "'Tis not Egypt, but Canada our masters will take us to. Egypt is across the seas. Father only means that we are to be enslaved like the Israelites. Remember Joseph?"

Eunice nods. They have read the story of Joseph just days ago. Standing there shivering in the snowy woods, she imagines a hot desert country with shining palaces and endless golden fields. She looks at Stephen and over toward her father bending his head to her mother, who now has little Warham by the hand.

"The Pharaoh was good to Joseph," she says, looking again at the stately savages never far from her father's side. "He was the Pharaoh's favorite."

The volleys of gunfire they heard earlier from a skirmish going on in the hay meadow, the very meadow Eunice and Stephen ran through with such abandon after the fall haying, have died away. The French and Indians who are still able have crossed the river now to join the rest. No one is left in Deerfield to give them chase.

CHAPTER 5

By the time their masters make camp on the second night, Eunice is beyond grief or pain. She is grateful to find beds of balsam boughs and blankets in a swiftly constructed wigwam after spending the first night shivering in the open. Indeed, it was a marvel to watch the smooth efficiency with which their masters erected the wigwams, the half-light of evening setting the snow to glowing. Since the Reverend Williams's prayers by the hill, they have traveled farther north than Eunice has ever been before, always with an eye to the rear, all of them half expecting their compatriots to overtake them. As the twilight deepens and this strange woodland town springs up, she clings to the hope that a militia will come in the night to save them.

What little food there is, most of it plundered from Deerfield, is shared. Eunice recognizes one of Parthena's apple cakes. They had baked so many for the baby's christening that the house had smelled of apples for days. Tears roll down her cheeks as she eats her small portion, but she is barely aware of them except as a warm tickle that leaves a cool trail. Her father, lying next to her with his wrists and ankles bound again, seems lost in his own somber thoughts, oblivious to her existence though they lean into each other for warmth. The smell of the balsam comforts her, but the cold is penetrating. Their masters make no fire. And again they are separated from the rest of their family. Her mother, Stephen, Esther, Samuel, and Warham are with other masters.

Dreams wind their way through her anxious sleep in the crowded wigwam. Eunice hears Parthena telling a lulling tale of a little girl on a warm, sunny island who, somewhere along the way, turns into her brother John playing marbles by the fire in Deerfield. Yet even as she dreams, she feels the cold and smells the pungent balsam they sleep on and the musky blankets and animal skins that cover them and knows that they are in the wilderness. The howling of the wolves mixes with the songs and shouts of a group of savages somewhere not far off.

In the morning spirits are very low. No food is offered or eaten by anyone before they set out again. Eunice sees Samuel and Warham at a distance, but she and her father are prevented from going to them before they set out on the next leg of their journey. Nor is there any sign of her mother or of Esther and Stephen. After their long ordeal of the previous day, her father is lame in one foot. He is limping and stumbles more frequently than yesterday.

"Mother must be behind us," Eunice thinks. "Since we go so slowly, we may fall back to where she is."

But this time, when her father loses his footing they are taken aside by their masters and joined by a third man with two long feathers bound into his hair and hanging down one side of his dark narrow face, accentuating the sharp planes of his blue-streaked cheekbones. He is lean and tall, and, again, Eunice thinks of the

Egyptians in the Bible. Could they look like this? There is some discussion among the men, and, gesturing toward her father, one of them points to his leg and mimics his limping gait. A French soldier who has stopped with them moves closer to listen, then whispers something to her father. The Reverend lets Eunice slide from his back, putting a hand on her shoulder, whether to steady himself or her, she isn't sure. His voice sounds as choked as it did when he was pushed into her dark bedroom in Deerfield.

"Eunice, our masters have seen that I cannot succeed in carrying you much farther." Her father pauses, casting about for words. Eunice looks up at him in terror, seeking out his eyes, but he seems to stare at the snow-covered ground as if it might offer an escape from what he has to say. She has to strain to hear him as he continues. "This man offers to carry you. He is Maqua, I think. These others," and he gestures toward the two he has called his masters, "are Huron. They come from farther north. We must thank the Lord you are protected." Her father's lips are drawn together in a thin line. "God willing, we will be together."

Immediately the long-feathered one, as Eunice thinks of him, squats down to be on Eunice's level. He smells of animal fat and smoke. Placing a hand on her shoulder, the savage looks closely into her face as, fighting her fear, she looks sideways at him. He puts his other hand to his chest uttering a strange word followed very clearly by "carry," and sweeps her onto his back, pulling a red and green blanket around her like a sling and fastening it across his chest. Suddenly she is more secure than she has been since they left Deerfield. As they start back into the grim line of travelers, Eunice searches again for her mother, hoping that their delay might have allowed her to catch up, but she sees no sign of her. As the savage who carries her picks up his pace, she struggles to look back to her father, but she is caught up too securely in the blanket that binds her to the savage's back.

As evening comes on, their masters spread out to make camp again. Eunice looks around in vain for her family as she shivers in the little clearing her master has made for her to rest in while he assembles a wigwam. She has not laid eyes on her father since they were separated. Two Deerfield men stumble from the woods, featureless as the dark tree trunks against the glowing snow. Arms pinioned behind their backs, they lurch up the incline toward her. They are talking in low, breathless voices, and her heart pounds wildly as she hears one of them say her mother's name. But she cannot be sure, and they are so intent on making their way across the crusty snowfield without use of their arms that they do not notice Eunice huddled against a tree trunk. A combination of fear, the heavy snow, and a weakness in her legs from being carried so long prevents her from trying to catch up to them to find out what they know of her mother.

When the men have passed, it occurs to Eunice that she could find her mother if she tried. She looks over to where the savage works on the wigwam and gingerly begins to test her legs. She pulls the rancid blanket the savage has given her tight around her shoulders and carefully begins to retrace her steps, thinking her mother must still be behind. The light is disappearing now, but she is sure that she can find her. She changes direction a little when she sees a fire through the trees, and begins stumbling as she loses caution, thinking only that she will find her mother now. She doesn't make a sound when a figure emerges from the trees to block her path and lifts her into his arms. Eunice struggles furiously, but dissolves in his powerful grip. She stares at the savage in terror until she can make out in the dark that he is the same man who has carried her all day. Somehow, in her certainty of finding her mother, it had seemed that he would disappear when she walked away. It had seemed as if she was walking home and that all she left behind in the woods would be gone. The savage silently carries her back to the shelter he has constructed for the night.

It is not until later the following day, when they stop at a camp on the Connecticut River, where their captors get food, sleds, and a pack of dogs they must have left behind before the attack, that Eunice sees any of her family again. It is here, amid the confusion of barking dogs and wounded Indians being strapped to sleds, that Eunice learns of her mother's death.

"I had a chance to pray with her, Eunice. She told me she wouldn't be able to go on. She is with John and Jerusha in heaven now. That thought was a comfort to her."

Her father seeks her eyes, but Eunice will not look. When she finds her voice, it doesn't sound like her own. "My mother?" is all she can say.

"My masters would not let me stay with her. She fell into the river—"

Her father tries to tell her more, but she will not hear it. She has heard snatches during the day—someone falling into an icy river, someone led away and murdered. She closes her eyes tight as her father speaks to her. She closes her eyes so tight that she sees the golden fields of Egypt. When she presses her fists to her eyes she sees a red sun glowing. Eunice stops her ears by screaming silently at her helpless father, "Be gone! Be gone! Be gone!"

. . .

She loses count of the days spent traveling on the long-feathered one's back. Wrapped snugly in the heavy blanket as if in a sack, she has been surprisingly comfortable. She hardly thinks about the smell of the blanket and the man. His gait is uneven because of the width of his snowshoes, but there is a lulling rhythm to it. Mostly the sky is gray as they head north. To Canada, she has often heard her elders say. But there are no longer any elders. Several weeks ago, after picking up dogs, sleds, and other supplies at the joining of two rivers, the French and the various tribes began to head in different directions before sorting themselves into smaller bands again. One day, she realizes that she can't remember when she last saw Warham or who his master was, for he had changed hands frequently. But she knows it has been many days since she last laid eyes on her little brother. With a stab of pain she understands that Stephen and his master are gone too. So are Samuel, Esther, and her father. Are they not all to go to Canada?

Their group is small since they took leave of the others. No adults from Deerfield remain, and most of the other children have parted from them too. Joanna Kellogg, Stephen's friend, remains with her band, which comforts Eunice though they are not allowed to talk very often. She has always looked up to eleven-year-old Joanna, who is pretty, capable, and easy with other people. And there are several other children. Sometimes they travel as a group, and sometimes Eunice is alone with her master. Each time the group breaks up, Eunice wonders if she will ever see the others again and thinks of her family killed and dispersed. She sometimes finds herself thinking that she will tell her mother about some small kindness the long-feathered savage has done for her, and then her mind is silenced. One of the savages killed her mother, or did she drown? And they took John, and the baby, and Parthena too. But are they dead? Eunice isn't sure.

The weather has turned warmer as March progresses, which

makes the going slippery for the men and the older children, who were given snowshoes when they stopped for supplies. Eunice envies the way they move freely, if clumsily, over the snow. She can make little progress on her own in the deep, soft snow, and must still be carried on her master's back or pulled on the sleds by the dogs. She loves the dogs. Even on warmer days she cannot hold on to a sled for long, so her survival depends on her master's willingness to carry her. She is sometimes afraid, but mostly she feels so snugly cocooned that she can't imagine any harm coming to her. She feels strangely safe, and sometimes it seems there is a voice telling her that all will be well.

The hunting has been fairly good, but meals are irregular, and she is often so hungry that she doesn't mind the lack of variety or the bloodiness of the hastily cooked meat. She falls hungrily on whatever is offered, sharing only the tiniest scrap with a dog with feathery brown and white fur and one blue eye who seems to have become attached to her. Sometimes they stop in the Indian villages or at the French forts they pass, and her master trades small pelts or loot from Deerfield for game. Eunice is amazed to find the wilderness so thoroughly peopled with villages. Strange that she had once imagined the hostile Indians streaming out of an empty wasteland. Of course they must have come from somewhere, must have a world of their own.

Tonight Eunice watches her master curiously as he sits on his heels building a fire. She passes kindling to him wordlessly, anxious for the fire to burn down so they can roast their meat. The dog stays close, as eager for food as Eunice is. They have eaten only parched corn for days. Eunice's face flushed crimson yesterday when her master returned silently, empty-handed, from checking his snares only to come upon her rummaging for the maple sugar candy that he seems to pull out of nowhere when she least expects it. She was both angry and ashamed. But the man threw back his head and laughed when he saw what she was doing. Not long afterward, he approached her with his hands hidden beneath his blanket. Withdrawing his closed fists he motioned for her to choose one and opened the fist she chose, disclosing a small brown lump of maple sugar.

"*Wakyen*," he said, gesturing for her to take it. And she was surprised once more that he thought about what she wanted and was not angry but gave it to her.

She still thinks of him as the long-feathered one, but he has taught her to call him Atironta. He has spread a small fur by the fire for her to sit on. The dog Atironta calls Tsihon (named, she thinks, for her one blue eye) settles beside her with a sigh. Sometimes in her sleep Eunice imagines for a moment her sister is with her, though it is only Tsihon at her side keeping her warm. Atironta treats Eunice kindly, but she is still fearful. He is her only support in the wilderness. He might decide she is too heavy or that he doesn't have enough food for her. Then she comforts herself. Sometimes the savages return their captives. After all, the Belding family was returned to Deerfield. How long will he keep her? And what will Canada be like? There is a sick feeling in the pit of her stomach that almost defeats her hunger.

Atironta looks up at her now with a small smile. Firelight shimmies up the bark walls of the wigwam as the fire springs to life. Their group has taken to scattering for days at a time to find game. The two of them came upon this wigwam the day before. Atironta showed her signs—a recent fire, some footprints heading away from the trail, a notch in a tree—that the remains of a recent kill might be buried in the snow nearby. Eunice was so hungry that she barely stopped to wonder whose house it was or what might happen if the owner returned.

Atironta looks up from the fire where he warms his hands and gestures toward the piece of venison they found buried not far from the wigwam and the sticks Eunice has sharpened while he cut the meat into chunks.

"*Wakahtas, kadon.*" His eyes smile, crinkling at the corners. *Wakahtas,* she understands from the way Atironta rubs his stomach, means eating a lot or filling one's belly, and *kadon* seems to be added after many statements to emphasize a meaning or a feeling. It is a word she hears often.

"*Ok'e,*" she responds in the word of assent she has learned from him. She threads the meat onto the sticks, not knowing whether it is his words or the routine that she understands.

• • •

As they come into the north country, the skeletal maple, oak, and hickory give way to immensely tall pines, their green branches brightly dappled with heavy clots of snow falling in little showers as they pass. *Iokeren'en,* says Atironta for the falling snow. As the silent hours of the trek pile up, the pines begin to seem like inscrutable beings to Eunice. Atironta names some of them for her, *ohtsokoton,* the balsam branches they use to make their beds, *onerahtase'kowa,* the tall white pine. She begins to understand how the words are put together. *Kowa* at the end of any word means it is big or great like the white pines that seem most alive to her. After so many weeks, the howling of the wolves at night, once terrifying, has come to seem more like crooning.

When Eunice and Joanna are in camp together one day, they watch Atironta open several pouches of red and blue powder. Holding the blue powder in his left hand, he begins mixing it into a paste with snow, gesturing to his own streaked cheekbones and then to Eunice's and Joanna's, repeating a word, *oronia*, that could mean the paint or their faces. It is hard to tell, but it is clear what he intends to do. Joanna looks terrified, then turns to Eunice.

"The paint is blue," she says. "It isn't black. Black paint would mean we are marked for death. That's what my brother Joseph told me." Atironta does not interrupt them this time, but lets them speak English as he strokes blue paint on one side of each girl's face, so that Eunice has the feeling she is looking in a mirror as she sees Joanna's face painted first a startling blue on one side, then bright red on the other, just as her own is. Joanna is completely transformed, and she knows she must be too.

"It would be hard for anyone to know us now," says Eunice.

"You have lighter hair and eyes," says Joanna, pausing for a moment. "But mine are as dark as theirs."

Atironta seems to watch them with extra attention. For the first time, Eunice wonders if he understands more English than he lets on. Soon afterward she is separated from Joanna again.

When they meet again a few days later, Eunice feels as if the whiteness all around them has sifted into their minds. Painted like their masters, they know each other and yet are alien. They are children of Deerfield yet not the same. Hunger and tiredness have become conditions like the snow.

One evening Joanna Kellogg's master ranges farther than usual in his hunting and does not return to the encampment, while Atironta has walked down to a nearby stream. Sitting together on a log by the cooking fire, Eunice and Joanna have an opportunity to talk more freely.

"The wolves are not far off tonight," remarks Joanna. "Did you ever think you could be out among them without fear? I used to pull the covers over my head and tremble when I heard them howling, though I was safe in my bed at home." Eunice is sobered for a moment at the thought of home. "Are you afraid?"

Eunice shakes her head. It suddenly occurs to her that most of the time she is not. "The pine trees look so strange to me," she confides to Joanna. "They seem like wise old people. Sometimes I think they have something to say to me."

"I think they will say it in Maqua," says Joanna with a laugh. They sit watching caverns form and dissolve in the glowing embers under a roasting rabbit set on a spit.

"I see Deerfield in the fire. There is the meetinghouse." Joanna points with a stick. "And your house behind it. And there is mine."

"Do you want to be there?" asks Eunice, thinking of the unimaginable distance they have come.

Tears spill down Joanna's cheeks and she bites her lip. "There is no one there," she says. All at once Joanna pokes her stick into the fire. The two girls watch the scene crumble before them.

• • •

With Joanna's master away, they are allowed to sleep together in the wigwam, the dog Tsihon plowing between them for warmth. They awaken in the morning refreshed and with a sense that their dreams were woven together as they slept, speaking to each other of Deerfield and the wilderness, weaving their lives into an intricate pattern enfolding them both.

In the morning Joanna's master returns, and they go their separate ways. Riding once again on Atironta's back so that they can travel quickly, Eunice makes up her own language to fill the time, inventing words for all the different kinds of snow that she sees around her. She has a name for the gray-white of the melting snow that they have been slogging through for the past few days, for the rare glare of icy snow in the midday sun, and for the blue snow under the tall pines, intense as the sky when darkness is falling. There are also the white icicles cascading down the red rock faces, and the silver-white gleaming snow on the peaks rising around them. All are named. And there is more. Eunice could go on forever with the ghost white of the mountain tops, barely distinguishable from clouds in a gray sky, and the dappled white of a piney mountainside, like sugar sifted on cake. And there are papery birches too, peeled back in places to show the fleshy wood beneath their curled white skins. Eunice amuses herself as she rides on Atironta's back, running through her many names to see if she can remember them each time. She sometimes notices how much like Atironta's words they sound.

The sky also occupies Eunice. The dead are there. The good ones are. Her mother, John, baby Jerusha, and Parthena too. She cannot help thinking that she will see them soon. For now, they have surely been carried to God like Faithful in the *The Pilgrim's Progress*. There is a dazzling rift of blue in the clouds over the mountains. Where God looks out, Eunice thinks. Below the rift, right atop the mountains, is a series of smaller green-blue rifts where Eunice imagines her dead are safely sheltered, peering out to admire her progress in this beautiful, frozen land.

So she occupies herself, wrapped securely in her blanket on Atironta's back. She does not mind the cold. In fact she does not feel especially cold anymore. And when the snow drives against her, sticking on her eyelashes and stinging her face, she can withdraw into the skins lining her blanket like the turtle she caught by the pond last summer.

Well beyond the place Atironta calls *atongotahkon,* they skirt the shore of a frozen body of water so large she thinks it might be the ocean. By the time they reach the high plateau beyond it, her fear begins to leave her. Now, she finds herself feeling strangely at one with the landscape, and she sees that Atironta cares for her as her own mother would, making sure that she is warm and fed, and letting her feed and pet the dogs under his careful eye when they stop. She sometimes imagines that he is the wayfarer, Christian, from *The Pilgrim's Progress,* and that she is the burden he carries so patiently in the picture in her father's book.

· · ·

One morning Eunice awakens to the scent of roasting meat. Tsihon licks her face and whines a bit as Eunice realizes that she is alone in the wigwam. Never before on her long journey has she smelled meat cooking in the morning. From outside their wigwam, Atironta calls her to wake up. "*Satketsko,*" he says. The hollow rumbling in her stomach also urges her from her bed of balsam boughs, furs, and blankets. Wrapping a fur from the bed around her shoulders, she stumbles out of the wigwam into a dazzling morning. She has forgotten the name she invented for such whiteness. It has been such a rarity on their march. And never before have they slept until the sun is fully risen. The light has the soft ambient quality that comes in April when the snow, though deep, is slippery and dissolving, and Eunice can almost smell the green life quickening underneath.

As her eyes adjust to the brightness Eunice sees that the little band has grown again. Forgetting the good smells from the cooking fire, she feels her heart leap. Stephen! Father! She searches the group around the fire, but these are new people, all of them Maqua. And there are women among them.

Atironta strides over to her accompanied by a woman so tall and stately that she seems like a queen from the Bible.

"Kenniontie," Atironta tells her, taking the woman's hand. She kneels down on one knee, bringing her face to Eunice's level.

"A'onote!" she says bending down and placing a hand gently on Eunice's shoulder. "A'onote," she repeats. "*Konyennetaghkwen.*" It is a word that Eunice understands to mean "my child."

The woman is dressed beautifully, wrapped in a dark cloak with fur inside and red and blue beadwork stitched along its edges in an intricate floral design. Her high cheekbones are painted with a spot of red, and her almond-shaped eyes look serious and kindly. She puts her other hand on her own chest. "Kenniontie!" she says, and looks up at Atironta with an unreadable expression. Then, addressing Eunice again, she says, "A'onote," and, rising, takes Eunice by the hand and leads her to the fire and the good-smelling food, asking if she is hungry, "*Satonhkaria'ks ken?*"

"*Nihawehkowa,*" answers Eunice, using one of the words she has learned for giving thanks, words repeated by Atironta every time they eat, like the grace her father said at home. The woman hands her a bowl of delicious stewed corn and meat, "*Onenhsto,*" the tall woman calls it. Eunice wolfs it down eagerly, feeding small pieces of meat to Tsihon, who has followed her.

"*Onenhstoiyo,*" Eunice tells her as she finishes. The stew is good.

There is talk and bustle around the fire as the food is passed around. Everyone eats. The newcomers begin taking apart the wigwams, putting the poles and other supplies back on the sleds for the dogs to pull. Eunice notices older children among them, some Stephen's age, and looks at them curiously, her mind numbed by her longing and her inability to ask about her brother. She would not know how to describe him.

The woman, Kenniontie, does not help the other new arrivals with their packing but remains with Eunice while she eats, studying her quietly and occasionally speaking to her. She points to the north and says, "Kahnawake," which Atironta has done too. But Eunice doesn't understand what Kahnawake is. The woman seems as kind as Atironta. Still, as Eunice's gaze moves from one group to another, she sees that Joanna and her master are no longer among them. The tall woman is gesturing to her, but Eunice hardly notices. She wants only to find Joanna.

The woman—"Kenniontie," she says again—helps her strap on a pair of snowshoes, *kahwenkare*, Eunice knows to call them now. They are not as easy to walk in as they appear. Eunice finds herself falling about like a toddler. Kenniontie laughs and helps her up again and again. She is patient and good-humored and seems in no rush to get anywhere. She shows her how to place her feet. Eunice even begins to laugh a little at her own clumsiness. How good it feels to laugh! The sense of urgency that has dogged them through the long march begins to dissolve in the sunshine. Eunice learns quickly and soon moves slowly but steadily alongside her new companion. The dog, Tsihon, released from sled duties, runs ahead, frisking and plowing with her nose in the snow.

The April sun has the warmth of springtime in it. Eunice feels it on her head and back despite the snow. The broad river is thinly iced, and as the day passes into afternoon the ice begins to glow an iridescent pink, until finally they reach a rapids, where all the ice is rough and broken. The day is growing colder, and Eunice has the feeling that she has entered into a wholly different world. Finally, through the trees, she makes out a village or fort, much bigger than the town of Deerfield, surrounded by a wood stockade set on high ground above the wild rapids. The woman who walks beside her smiles and says again, "Kahnawake."

PART II

CHAPTER 6

A heavy smell of bodies, smoke, and meals past underlies a fresher scent. The lighter scent is so familiar that Eunice's eyes prick with tears. She closes them, shutting out the strangeness, summoning a summer day, Parthena gathering up her hair, working at the knots with her comb. *Sit still for a moment, Eunice, you wiggle like a tadpole!* But her lilt slides into the grave melody of another language, murmured soothingly among strange women.

The striped trade blanket is rough against the goosey chill of Eunice's skin. She huddles in its thick folds and blinks away the scrim of tears that has surprised her. Her nakedness beneath the blanket makes her feel weak and vulnerable, and her limbs feel peculiarly loose. She studies the dim interior. Pale gray afternoon light filters through a hole in the ceiling. The house is different from the wigwams she slept in throughout most of her journey and unlike most of the cabins she passed when they entered the settlement at Kahnawake. It is long and narrow, like a covered bridge overlaid with rough elm bark. She looks toward the posts at the entrance, tall, rough, deeply carved with a pattern of ovals. They seem matched somehow to the stately woman who has brought her here. The woman has taken off her elaborate robe to reveal a simple tunic with deer-hide leggings underneath. Eunice tries unsuccessfully to recall her name.

Adjusting to the dimness, Eunice examines in more detail the swathes of wampum, copper plates, and carved wood that hang on the walls. On one of the posts is a cradle board with intricate floral carvings and blue and white beaded straps hanging down. On the floor there are mats woven of rush, and small mortars filled with crushed yellow-green buds are set around the hearthstones.

Two women, who earlier brought bowls of warm water for rubbing away the dirt and thick pigment that had streaked Eunice's face throughout her journey, now settle themselves on either side of her. One is very old, and the other young. The older one, a woman with a deeply lined and pockmarked face, is arranging bright beads on a shiny black ribbon, not looking at her. Eunice has never seen anyone so old. The woman's eyes recede into weathered folds, and her wrinkled face resembles an apple figure that Parthena once carved so that the features shrank and withered when it dried. Her mother had been upset when she saw it, but never said a word about it to the Reverend. The old woman focuses all her attention on the beads, plucking them neatly from a wooden bowl with long, strong fingers and laying them out on the ribbon. The younger woman stands holding a tangled net at arms' length to inspect it for breaks in its diamond pattern, and then settles in to begin mending it. The girl looks over her shoulder at the one who brought her here. *Kenniontie,* she repeats silently, relieved to remember, and turns curiously to the colorful line of beads as the old woman begins to thread them onto another twisted ribbon. Her clothes are dun colored, and her skin has a luminous burnished texture despite its many wrinkles. A child's cry pierces the quiet, and the younger woman drops her net and hurries to the far end of the room. A moment later she returns, settling the little boy at her breast.

"*Kajatoreton*," says the old woman. Eunice understands that she wants to see the silver cup that she clutches beneath her blanket. She withdraws it from the folds uneasily. There is something irresistible in the steady gaze of this ancient person. She begins to extend the cup, but when the woman reaches out a long, dry hand to take it, Eunice snatches it back. The hand seems to her like a strange thing with a life all its own. Eunice's cry of alarm startles the nursing child, who jerks his head from his mother's breast and stares at her with round black eyes. "*Oghniyawenhonh?*" he asks.

"Shhh! *Ohnwatsihon*," soothes his mother. The child continues to stare for a moment before nuzzling his way under the tunic again.

Kenniontie hurries across the room. The women confer briefly, and she seats herself.

"A'onote," she says, gesturing toward the cup and then toward Eunice. Kenniontie closes Eunice's hand over her treasure before settling down beside her. "Asientie," says Kenniontie, looking toward the old woman as she says her name. "Sientiesie. Ohnwatsihon." She indicates the young woman and her baby.

Kenniontie pulls Eunice's hair off her neck, gently rubbing away the remains of red paint that cling there. She dips a rag in the warm water, wringing it out so that the water will not run down Eunice's neck and make her shiver as she rubs the last bit of red pigment from around her ear. Eunice begins to feel better as Kenniontie works warm oil into her hair and weaves the bright beads she takes from Asientie's hand into a few strands, the name A'onote recurring like a little wave lapping on the shore as she speaks quietly to the other women.

Eunice is fascinated by a chest with elaborate floral designs carved into it and a stain of some kind that makes the flowers red. The carving swirls in a way that makes the flowers look alive, and she notices a bird among the vines that looks as if it could fly right off. Kenniontie stops her work, a braid held in one hand, and runs her fingers over the design on the chest.

"*Keronto*, A'onote," says Kenniontie, naming the chest, and she gestures that Eunice should explore the design too.

"*Ok'e*," Eunice answers and runs her fingers over its smooth and twisting lines, listening to the words for bird, leaf, and vine, which she has heard before from Atironta. She repeats the names again as she traces them. After many weeks of traveling with Atironta, not only are many of the words becoming familiar to her, but the sounds of the language seem familiar too. Atironta has told her that both the language and his people are called Canienga. They do not call themselves Maqua as the French and many English people do. They call themselves the Canienga, "People of the Flint."

The woman with the little boy lays a beaded dress and a pair of red leggings next to a conch shell that sits on top of the chest. The tunic is midnight blue, made of a rich, heavy cotton, its sleeves trimmed with red ribbon. On the deep-blue ground, fancy beadwork stars, grass green and pink, surround a delicate beadwork tree of peace in the center. The clothes are beautiful, unlike any she has seen before. No, she thinks. They are like the robe Kenniontie wore earlier in the day, but they look like they might be her own size. Kenniontie doesn't say anything, but looks at the beaded clothes and back at her, until Eunice can no longer keep her curiosity to herself.

"*Sahtsheronnianion*, A'onote," says Kenniontie, and she gestures for her to get dressed.

Eunice is not sure what to do. The women seem to wait, but she doesn't see how she can keep the blanket around her, hold on to her cup, and dress herself all at once. Although the same women helped her take off her old clothes and washed her earlier, she doesn't want to shed the blanket in front of them. At home she rarely took off her petticoat even to wash. Finally, the women turn away. Even so, she struggles to get the dress on before dropping the blanket, quickly snatching up her cup when she gets the leggings on. The dress is a little too big for her, but it feels soft, and looking down at it, she loves the beads. Kenniontie helps her tie the cup to a loop at the side of the red leggings. Eunice's eyes fill with tears, which spill over and run down her cheeks this time. She sees that Kenniontie means well, but she does not want her to touch the cup her mother gave her.

•   •   •

The next day, Eunice, wearing a fur vest over her brilliant beaded tunic, traces patterns of lichen on a large rock not far from the entrance to the house. Every once in a while she looks up to watch billowing white clouds roll across the sky. Heaven is behind them. If she looks long enough, she might catch a glimpse of it. All at once, she hears a series of sharp explosions. She jumps down from the rock. Gunshots, she thinks, and her heart begins pounding. She could slip into the nearby orchard to hide and watch. Her father and Samuel might be coming with a brigade like the ones she used to watch at practice on the parade grounds at Deerfield; torn between running and listening, she looks back at the carved posts that frame the door of the house. Perhaps her eldest brother,

Eleazer, has come from Boston, or it might be other English people that she would recognize. She can feel her heart beat slowly, heavily, almost in her throat. She pictures her father's high forehead and blue eyes, and her throat tightens. Would she know if it was Eleazer? He seems as indistinct to her as the faraway city where he lives. The world seems to crack in two again with another round of thunder.

"A'onote."

She is starting into the orchard when she turns to the sound of her new name. Atironta stands between the carved doorposts of the longhouse, shading his eyes with his hand. He appears unalarmed when she begins to turn away from him, and he calls her again. The young orchard is patchy with unmelted snow. Eunice takes a few uncertain steps but is now aware that she has no idea what she is walking toward. In the doorway is safety.

"Guns?" she asks, walking toward him and mimicking the pulling of a trigger, though she thinks he will know this word in English.

He shakes his head to reassure her but has difficulty explaining the sound. He runs his fingers along like flowing water and says the word for brook. This she understands. But when he brings his hands up and smacks his fist into his palm, she can make no sense of it.

"Fighting?" she asks. Atironta shakes his head again.

Finally, Atironta gathers his fishing gear and beckons for her to follow him. She hesitates for a moment. But Atironta has made it clear that there is no fighting. He calls to Tsihon and takes her a long way up the brook that runs along the far side of an orchard of saplings before emptying into the rapids.

Eunice stands in the dewy cold, regarding the field of white, broken at the center by braided black water. Atironta beckons again, and they continue to where a waterfall rushes over a rocky shelf, playing behind a thin wall of ice with an eerily dancing light. Suddenly she hears and then sees for herself a whole section of ice heave and shatter. Not guns; there is no one coming for her. Not now, anyway. When will they come, she wonders. And will there be fighting? She remembers what Joanna Kellogg told her about how the Maqua—the Canienga, she corrects herself—use captives to bargain with. Will they trade her for someone else, one of their own people? And what about the rest of her family? Who will do the bargaining? She has seen no one from home since she arrived in this place and wonders if Joanna is in a longhouse like Kenniontie's or one of the square houses, which seem to be more common in Kahnawake.

The strange effect of the delicate ice wall is destroyed as huge shards of ice hang for a moment before plunging over the falls into the running stream below. In a black pool set apart from the main stream, some kind of small animal whirls, sucked under and pulled back up at the edge. It draws her eye, yet makes her queasy. She can't tell what it is. Guns kill, but water kills too, she thinks.

Atironta's voice pulls her away from the disturbing pool. He smiles the crooked, wolfish smile that comes when he is pleased with some enterprise, looking up at her from beneath his winged brows, dark eyes crinkling. And he beckons her to a more peaceful stretch upstream from the waterfall. Eunice watches her beaded moccasins pressing into the lace of the disappearing snow, pale beads punctuated with blood-red ones, like winter berries. She is aware of how comfortably her feet are cradled, cushioned, and kept warm by a thick layer of dried grass inside her new moccasins, so much softer than her old leather slippers. A grove of tiny hemlock seedlings pushes its way through the snow, dark green and perfect, a tiny version of the woods they walk through. She tries not to step on them, for they seem part of some tiny alternate world that she cannot see.

They stop and Atironta begins to unfold a net. How, she wonders, will he secure it? The ice is uncertain, and the stream fast with spring melt. He cannot easily reach the other shore. She watches as he makes a loop and then another in the ropes that extend from the top and bottom of his net, tying them together at the base. He motions for her to sit beside him and gives her some bark strips, showing her how to further secure and stiffen each loop separately. Her hands are red and cold, but not too cold to follow his motions. Finally, Atironta motions for her to stand. He takes the loops and tosses them toward the branch thrust up from a fallen tree a little way out in the ice. Missing his mark, he pulls the net back, turning to her with the loops.

"A'onote." He guides her tosses until the loop slides over the branch. Picking up his fishing spear, he extends it until he can delicately sever the pieces of rope that hold the loops together. He shakes the net out until it falls into the moving water, spreading out to take its catch. It is not long before Atironta gestures to Eunice to help him pull in the net, which is full of young salmon, some large trout, and an eel that nearly slithers through. Pleased, Atironta skins the eel immediately.

An hour later, they return to the longhouse, a strip of eel skin strung through the gills of the fish, which Atironta had swiftly killed, showing Eunice how to force the jaw back with a thumb to break the fish's spine. There are strangers standing outside the longouse with Kenniontie: a Kahnawake girl about her own age and a man whom Atironta greets heartily.

"A'onote." Kenniontie takes Eunice by the hand as she pulls the other girl forward. "Gaianniana." Eunice repeats the name to remember it. She does not hear the man's name, but she thinks he must be the girl's father. Gaianniana is taller than Eunice and wears an emerald green tunic with red and blue beadwork. She does not look very happy to be visiting, but she pulls from her pouch a doll made of cornhusks and dressed in blue and red clothes like Eunice's with green and pink beads sewn on. She holds it out to Eunice, gesturing for her to take it, but she does not smile or even greet Tsihon, who nudges her hand and wags her tail.

"*Nihawehkowa.*" Eunice thanks her, but she wishes Joanna Kellogg had come to visit her instead. She wonders where Joanna has been taken. The visitors do not stay long, and she is relieved when they go. She cannot imagine that this girl will be a friend to her.

CHAPTER 7

A week passes before Eunice meets Gaianniana again. She catches sight of her one afternoon coming with her father, Onwekowa, from the more densely settled part of the village toward Kenniontie's house. Eunice watches her making playful feints at a pack of hungry dogs begging treats at her heels. As they come closer, her father reaches into a pouch at his waist for a strip of dried meat and berries, the pemmican these people seem always to carry.

"*Kannonhoeron*, A'onote," the father greets her. But Gaianniana hangs back until her father motions her to step forward. He hands her some pemmican and calls the dogs. Gainniana makes them sit, so she can feed them, naming each dog before giving it its treat. The father, a big, handsome, generous-looking man, nudges Gaianniana. She turns to Eunice and holds out the rest of the pemmican to her, and as Eunice takes her turn at feeding the dogs, names them again for her. Tsihon comes around from behind the house, where she has been sleeping in the sun.

"Tsihon," says Eunice, introducing her own dog. She is glad to see even a stranger her own age, but Gaianniana seems to stare at the beadwork tree on Eunice's tunic and says nothing until her father prods her again.

"Tsihon," repeats Gaianniana. There is no friendliness in her voice, and under her breath she mutters, "Guerrefille," looking hard at Eunice, who knows only that the word has something to do with Deerfield.

Suddenly, the old woman, Asientie, is at Eunice's side, a hand on her shoulder, her hooded eyes holding the other girl's.

"Gaianniana, *atere!*" says Asientie, "*Nihawehkowa.*" She seems to thank her for something. Satisfied, she continues speaking to Gaianniana as if no one else exists for her. Eunice hears her Kahnawake name, "A'onote," several times and also the words for some plants she has heard named before. The old woman gestures toward the orchard beyond the house, and Eunice hopes she is sending the girl on some errand. But Asientie nods toward Eunice and gestures that the girls should go together.

"A'onote!" Gaianniana tosses the name curtly over her shoulder, the way Atironta might call Tsihon.

Eunice, still wary, gathers her courage and whistles for Tsihon, who has gone back to lie in the sun. Immediately Tsihon, sensing adventure, comes racing toward the girls.

"*Kannonhoeron,* Tsihon!" Eunice greets her dog, who runs in circles around them, then settles down expectantly. This time Gainniana bends to stroke Tsihon's head and exclaims at her varicolored eyes. Eunice understands this. Most people comment on her dog's unusual blue and brown eyes, sometimes wondering if the dog is blind, for the brown in one eye is shot through with blue as if by a bolt of light.

Eunice nods with pleasure when Gaianniana says the dog is pretty. Her companion seems a little less intimidating, though her look is still guarded. She continues to stroke the dog, pulling more pemmican from her pouch. Eunice tries to swallow her uneasiness. It is nice to see someone her own age, but she can see that this girl has not chosen to be with her.

They are going to look for some plants. This she has understood from Asientie. But where or how far they are going, A'onote has no idea. The houses in Kahnawake, at least twice as many as there were in Deerfield, it seems to Eunice, are set in groves of small, crabbed trees and have dirt tracks between them. She is uneasy as they approach the stockade fence that surrounds the village, the only part of Kahnawake that reminds her of Deerfield. She had not expected that they could leave the settlement on their own.

"*Dhatkonkoghdaghkwanyanken?* We are going out?" she manages to ask. Each time anyone of her longhouse passes through the door they repeat the word *atongotahkon* for her benefit. A'onote is proud of how quickly she has learned to put some of the words together.

"We are going to gather greens by the river, *kadon*," replies Gaianniana, bending to pick some grass and running her fingers along like water to show her meaning as she speaks. Eunice understands without the gesture. The words for river and greens are used so often, they too have become familiar.

They do not head for the big rapids that they see from the settlement's edge. They are heading down an incline in the opposite direction. Eunice wonders whether the girl could be leading her astray. She looks up, and the sky is flat and endless, cold and without the light that suggests God's presence. She cannot imagine her mother there.

Gaianniana gives a snort of pleasure as Tsihon races ahead and then back to them.

"Tsihon! She is well named, *kadon*. She is truly very swift."
She slides one hand off the other in a gesture indicating speed
and looks inquiringly into A'onote's eyes to see if she understands her.

"Tsihon?" repeats Eunice, pointing to her own eye questioningly. Perhaps she has been mistaken about the meaning of her
dog's name.

Gaianniana shakes her head and makes the gesture for speed
again.

"Tsihon!" says Eunice, mimicking Gaianniana's gesture with a
bewildered laugh, realizing that her dog's name is not "Blue" but
"Swift."

Suddenly, the dog returns at full speed again, nearly bowling
them over, leaving the two girls laughing with surprise.

"Tsihon," Eunice repeats. "*Kadon.*"

They have reached an area of level ground. Gaianniana suddenly turns sharply to the right, beckoning to Eunice as she heads
toward a spot where a path opens up through a thicket of trees.
They emerge on a promontory just beyond the stockade, surrounded by cedars and looking out over the tossing silvered rapids
far below.

"*Onen'takwententsera,*" Gaianniana says quietly. She seems to
be offering the place like a gift as, for the first time, she looks
directly into Eunice's eyes. Then she turns away and sets off at a
faster pace back through the thicket, heading away from the big
river once again. Eunice lingers for a moment before picking up her
pace to catch up to the stalwart figure ahead of her. She has only a
glimmering of what Gaianniana has said. It has to do with the place,
returning to it. She looks at Gaianniana's back where her dark hair
swings against her emerald tunic. Tsihon and this clearing seem to

have dispelled Gaianniana's surliness entirely. It seems possible that they will be friends.

. . .

It rains for several weeks after Eunice's visit to the cedars with Gaianniana. On the first clear day, Eunice looks up from the stick she is whittling as she sits on a rock outside the longhouse. She squints down the sun-spangled path, recognizing the approaching figure before she can fully make it out.

"*Dewadadenonweronne*, A'onote!" Come! Gaianniana calls out to her.

Eunice looks down again and continues paring a stick with a knife given to her by Atironta. She wants to make it as smooth as the dolls he carved for her before setting out on a trading expedition early in the Planting Moon. Kenniontie has shown Eunice the seeds—corn, squash, beans, which she calls "the three sisters that sustain us"—and how she and the other women will plant a combination of the seeds in the small mounds of earth they have prepared in the fields in and around Kahnawake. The smoothing of the stick soothes Eunice, and she can hardly bear to release herself from the project, which has helped her avoid the empty sky above, the clouds wispy, no shape to fix a thought on.

It is a relief to sit outside in the sun after the last few weeks in the smoky longhouse. It has been an unseasonably cold and rainy spring until now, and cooking fires had to be made indoors. Eunice's eyes are still red and irritated from the smoke that filled the house instead of rising through the smoke holes. The smoke made her throat ache, and one morning she woke up in terror with her eyes swollen almost shut. When Kenniontie tried to bathe them in warm water with some kind of herb, Eunice irritably pushed her hand away. She suddenly hated her, hated her tallness, her almond eyes, her severe beauty, and, above all, her kindness. What right had she? Finally, when Eunice could stand the burning and oozing no longer, she had allowed Asientie to bathe them. The swelling has gone down, but her eyes remain red and itchy. Now she rouses herself, puts her work aside, and slides down from the rock as Gaianniana comes closer.

"We'll go to the cedars," says Gaianniana grasping her hand. Eunice puts her stick and knife in a pouch and begins to rise, content to be distracted.

"Ohnwatsihon will come with us," Gaianniana says cheerfully, shooting her a sideways glance. "We can make a game to keep him busy, *kadon*."

"*Ai!*" exclaims Eunice, imitating cries of surprise she hears other children make. Her cheeks are burning. Eunice has forgotten she should be looking after Sientiesie's little boy, Ohnwatsihon, while the women are working in the fields. She has left him inside on his own, but Gaianniana seems to think this is funny and laughs, a clear, bell-like sound.

Before whistling for Tsihon, Eunice rushes in to Ohnwatsihon, who seems happy enough on his own and unaffected by the lingering smell of smoke. She takes his hand as he emerges from the longhouse, and they head across the village toward the opening in the stockade. Avenues of plum trees line the paths between the houses and litter the ground with pale petals. Eunice looks down at her moccasins on the soft, petaled path and imagines her stiff slippers on the rutted road in Deerfield.

Ohnwatsihon tugs gently on her hand. If she doesn't look, it could be Warham's hand in hers; she might even hear her mother's voice, or Parthena's, calling them. Her eyes, already red and runny,

begin to fill with tears. A fist forms in her throat as other images
begin to rise, eclipsing the world around her, leaving her awash
with misery, alone in the cool, gauzy light of an alien world. She
walks on, holding Ohnwatsihon's hand, hardly hearing, much less
understanding Gaianniana's bell-like prattle. When Tsihon comes
racing toward them, anxious as ever not to be left out, the knot in
Eunice's throat loosens a little. She sees her dog through a wash of
tears and claps her hands to welcome her.

They have come to a little stand of cedars surrounding a mossy
clearing. Gaianniana nudges Eunice, untying her cloth pouch to
reveal a supply of maple sugar lumps and pemmican.

"We'd better eat some now, *kadon*. Before they melt."

Ohnwatsihon reaches eagerly for his. Eunice, still dazed with a
double vision, takes hers and lets the sugar dissolve slowly in her
mouth. The shock of sweetness revives her spirits a little, but she
still feels an overwhelming sense of loss that even in her native
tongue she would not have words for.

Gaianniana takes from her pouch a handful of plum pits
painted white on one side and red on the other. "Look here," she
says and calling out "White!" she tosses the pits onto the bed of
soft pine needles, looking pleased when the white sides outnumber
the red by two. She places a pretty, green glass bead on the ground,
scoops up the pits, and hands them to Eunice to toss. Eunice
tosses the pits to compete for the bead. "Red!" she calls, and since
almost all the pits show their red side, Gaianniana gives her the
bead. They go on, getting Ohnwatsihon to find a feather, a nut, a
marbled stone for them to toss for until they grow tired of the
game. Gaianniana ties a pinecone to a low branch and gives him a
small pile of stones to throw at it, and the girls lie down to look at
the sky.

"So many games," says Eunice. "I've never learned so many before."

"Then what did you do?"

"We have dolls, like you do." Eunice shrugs and remembers all the lessons and chores that took up most of her time. Then she remembers the fort she built with Stephen. For a minute she almost hears John's voice, but she stops herself from thinking of that.

They pay only enough attention to Ohnwatsihon so that they can whoop happily with the boy on the rare occasions when he hits a swinging pinecone.

A flock of cedar waxwings twitters and whistles high in the branches above them where the light creates a shimmering green canopy. Gaianniana chatters away. Eunice, catching little more than half what she says, is content for now to let the fluting sound eddy around her. The tall, straight cedar trunks are a warm rosy color in the sunlight and the sun warms the backs of their loose tunics.

Ohnwatsihon laughs as he tries to hit the pinecone. Gaianniana is trying to aim his hand for him when she stiffens, clamping her hand over his mouth. The sound of men's voices penetrates the tree break. They call to each other in a strange language, neither Canienga nor English nor French. Eunice sits up and looks questioningly at Gaianniana, seeing right away that she looks frightened. They both look in terror at Ohnwatsihon. He will not know how to be quiet.

The path to their spot is barely discernible through the brush. Still, the slightest sound would give them away. Gaianniana is frantically untying her pouch while Eunice tries to distract the boy. There is one large lump of maple sugar and some pemmican left in the pouch. Making big eyes and putting her hand over her mouth in a sign for silence, Gaianniana pops the sugar lump into the little boy's mouth.

The birds continue their sociable chatter. The sun still shines so high above. The men's voices are lower now. They seem to have come together just beyond the tree break. How many? Eunice watches Gaianniana put her finger to her lips before each bite she offers her little cousin, smiling sweetly as if it is a game. Eunice wonders if she knows what kind of people they are that speak so strangely. A burst of short barks interrupts this thought, and a fresh shock of fear shoots through her. Tsihon is returning from her explorations. Eunice stifles the impulse to cry out for her dog, afraid both that the men will shoot Tsihon and that she will lead them to the cedars. Tsihon is growling now, not coming any nearer. Her intermittent growling and barking is punctuated by a shot. Eunice can barely stop herself from crying out in anguish. The men's talk goes on. Tsihon does not come. Even Ohnwatsihon seems to understand that something is wrong.

After what seems an endless time, the voices begin to recede down the slope. Eunice releases her breath and rises, edging toward the path, but Gaianniana grabs her arm. "You can't! They know that dogs travel with people."

Only when the voices have faded away does Tsihon come springing through the brush. Tears flood Eunice's eyes.

"Good girl, Tsihon!" Eunice whispers in relief. "And you, Ohnwatsihon, are a good man!" Both have protected them when they expected to be betrayed. Eunice lifts her hand to show Gaianniana how it is trembling. They giggle madly.

Gaianniana beckons toward a rocky outcropping beyond their little circle of cedars. Cautiously they creep out on the boulder and see, winding their way below them, the figures of five men, dressed in the English style. Eunice clings to the boulder as she watches them go, feeling the blood drain from her head. She clenches her jaw as her face goes ashen. They could be looking for me, she thinks; they might have come to take me home, and I have lost them. But they cannot be English, speaking such a strange-sounding language. It is impossible to know now.

CHAPTER 8

The next day, Gaianniana appears at the longhouse very early. Asientie greets her and calls to Eunice. Kenniontie has already left for one of the nearby fields inside the stockade. Now that it is clear she is to spend another day with Gaianniana, Eunice is almost pleased. As they leave the house, the sky to the east is pearly pink like the inside of the conch shell Asientie keeps on the chest in the longhouse. Clouds fan out above the pink like a white beach combed by waves. Tsihon gets up to follow, but Asientie calls her back. Tsihon has never before been kept from following her.

She looks questioningly to be sure Asientie means to keep Tsihon from coming. Asientie shakes her head. "Not this time," she says.

Eunice picks up the cornhusk doll she left outside the door the night before, when it got too dark to keep working on the stitches she was adding. She looks questioningly at Asientie once more, but it is Gaianniana who puts her palms together as if praying.

"To meeting?" asks Eunice, startled. But she says it in English, and Gaianniana doesn't understand her, just takes her hand. For a moment she imagines her father might be preaching at the meetinghouse. Then she remembers his words: "These people are Catholics and heathens, Eunice. You must remember your own prayers. You must not kneel to the Devil and his idols." And she has remembered her prayers. But how will she know if she is worshipping the Devil?

"Eunice!" Coming out of one of the square houses at the edge of the more densely settled part of the village, Joanna Kellogg calls out to her. She wears a dark tunic with pale quillwork down the front and green beads at the center. Her clothes accentuate her dark good looks. Joanna too is with a Kahnawake girl, or maybe not a girl. Eunice can't tell how old she is. She is plump and pretty and more grown-up looking than Joanna. Eunice knows she is not supposed to speak English here, but Joanna plunges ahead. "You look different," she says, gesturing toward Eunice's smooth, oiled hair and beaded clothes. "I must look different too." She shakes her head, as if this had not occurred to her before.

"I like the way you look," says Eunice.

"I haven't seen you with the priests before." She pauses, looking closely at Eunice. "I don't think the Latin prayers they teach can harm us, since we have no idea what they mean." Joanna Kellogg's smile dimples below the two red spots painted on her cheekbones, but Eunice's hand goes to the silver cup tied beneath her tunic. This must be what her father warned her of. She clutches her doll with the other hand as if to make up for the missing Tsihon.

Gaianniana tugs at Eunice's sleeve and shakes her head. She takes Eunice's hand and says firmly, "A'onote."

"You would not believe who I saw in the city of Montreal!" Joanna rushes on, ignoring what was clearly meant as a command to come along and stop speaking English. Her voice is rich with excitement. "'Twas Zebediah Carter. He was well, but longing for home. He heard that your father is with the priests in Quebec, and he has seen some others from home! God has preserved him.

Eunice has no idea how far Quebec might be. But Zebediah has seen her father!

"Did he know anything else of my family?" asks Eunice. Her heart lurches as she thinks of what might have happened to her brothers and sister.

"We didn't have much time to talk, but I think he would have told me if he had. If God has preserved your father, the others may be well." Eunice starts to ask about Joanna's family, but can't get a word in. "I have been working in the fields with the women; there was so much to do. Isn't it strange the way the women do the planting here? But I like it. I've never worked outside, except to fetch water. I am learning fancy beadwork for a dress. I want to show it to you." Joanna's words seem to tumble like a waterfall, from one ledge to another.

"What is it like in Montreal? Is it like home?" Eunice asks.

Joanna laughs. "Not a bit. It is not very far away from here, and so full of all kinds of people that it is beyond comparing to any town I have ever seen. It is true, what they say, that the buildings are very big, bigger and grander than I ever imagined, and they are made of stone. I do not think even Boston can be so big. There is one building so tall that you have to bend your neck way back to see the top. And what do you think? There is a clock they call *la horloge*! I cannot tell what is written on it, but it has two hands that move and a bell. The priests can read the time from it."

Gaianniana pulls more firmly on her hand now, leading her onto a well-worn path into the woods. Joanna and the other girl hang back before following, but Joanna calls out once more, "Perhaps we may meet around the village!"

It is not long before the woodland path brings them to another settlement, not quite as foreign looking as the Kahnawake village. There are none of the arbor-shaped longhouses of Kahnawake, but tall, square buildings with glass windows, like the houses back in Deerfield. Eunice does not remember, or at least cannot picture, her home in Deerfield burned to a pile of rubble. On the occasions when she allows herself to think of home, she imagines it as she knew it. When Gaianniana leads her into the largest house, the mission house she is told, it is not so unlike the Deerfield meetinghouse with its wide-board floors and beamed ceiling, though the heathen figures and the crosses she sees are just what her father warned her of. It is the differences enfolded in the sameness that are unsettling, for didn't her father say that the Devil puts on clever guises?

The man who approaches looks nothing like her father. Gaianniana presents Eunice to the priest, who wears flowing black robes and has a short, gray-flecked beard outlining a lean, square jaw. He is slighter than the Kahnawake men and very pale under his broad-brimmed black hat.

"Achiendase," says Gaianniana, indicating the priest.

"A'onote," he says, lifting Eunice's chin to look in her eyes. And then, "*kheien'a*," meaning daughter, which sends a shiver down Eunice's spine.

Achiendase turns to greet the other children as they enter and seat themselves, paying special attention to the English children scattered throughout the group. He seems to know Joanna Kellogg already.

"*Kheien'a*," he says again, taking Joanna's hand. He gestures for all the children to seat themselves on the benches he has placed in a large circle. Some do, but others, Eunice and Gaianniana among them, seat themselves on the floor.

In the center of the circle stands an easel with a painting that someone has been working on. In its background a cross stands on one side, and on the other stands an empty tomb. In the foreground there is a woman in blue robes with bright light radiating around her head.

"Oneyete Marie." The priest says. This woman in blue with the light around her head reminds Eunice of her own mother. It seems like a kind of magic. She cranes her neck to try to see Joanna's response. They are not supposed to worship pictures. Is that what this man wants them to do? But Joanna, on a bench behind her, is studying the picture carefully with a rapt look on her face, while Achiendase continues.

The somber black robe of the priest is stranger to her than Indian clothes, and it has none of their appeal. Surely, this is one of the men Eunice's father preached against, and she can imagine him as a devil. Hasn't she seen the priests in pictures with their billowing back robes and huge, brimmed hats? She remembers a picture of an evil crow enfolding a congregation in his blue-black wings.

"You are welcome here, A'onote." Achiendase says this in English, bending down to her. "This is for you." He offers her a whorled shell, just like Asientie's, but much smaller. "Are they good to you at Kahnawake?"

"Yes," she answers. She cannot say that they are not kind.

Achiendase asks to see her doll and admires the new stitches she has added to its dress.

There is another painting on one of the walls, as beautiful as the one on the easel. It reminds her of a portrait in the Carter's house of Mrs. Carter as a girl, standing with a green sheep's meadow in the background, the only painting in the town of Deerfield. The colors in this picture are both softer and brighter than the ones in the Carter's painting. It is hard to think of it as evil. She wonders whether looking at it is the same as worshipping it. There were no pictures in the meetinghouse at home, nothing to distract from her father's sermons and prayers.

"Kateri Tekakwitha," says the priest when he sees her looking at it. "She was a great and very holy healer, a saint of the Kahnawake people. Asientie knew her many years ago, when she was a young girl like you, but Kateri was taken to heaven long ago."

She does not have the light around her head in the picture. It might be better to look at this one. Though the other picture draws her to it, this one makes Eunice feel that she would like to cure the sick too. She would like to have the picture; even more, she would like to know how to make one.

Achiendase gives the children beads for learning prayers in Latin, the Devil's tongue. Their rhythm is soothing, and she cannot help enjoying them a little, just as she loves getting pretty beads for learning them. She has always been good at learning things by heart. Looking up at the window high above her, she sees on a leafy branch a bluebird with a blush of red on its breast and thinks for a moment that it must be her mother come to watch over her in this strange, unsettling world.

• • •

When Eunice returns to the longhouse at midday a week later to fetch some string for a game, Achiendase is seated outside, deep in conversation with Kenniontie, Atironta, and Asientie. Kenniontie's brothers, Tsiatekenha and Onwekowa, sit listening to her. The priest speaks earnestly, and Kenniontie keeps shaking her head. Smoke curls lazily from the smooth soapstone pipe they pass among them.

"You cannot refuse him this time," Achiendase continues in his faltering Canienga. "Onnontio, the Governor, gives you his pledge. A'onote can remain with you." Instead of returning to play, Eunice seats herself next to Kenniontie. She is not sure of all they say, but it concerns her. Kenniontie speaks quietly to Onwekowa before turning back to the priest.

"This child, A'onote, is planted with us," she says. "We would sooner part with our own hearts than with this child." She gestures toward Eunice and puts her hand to her heart.

Eunice's own heart flutters in her chest at this. She has heard of Onnontio, the French governor. Does he want to buy her away from them and give her back to her father or trade her away to someone else? She remembers what Mary Brooks told her about Parthena and Frank, that they could be traded like goods if her father wanted to trade them. But she understands what Kenniontie has said—that they would sooner part with their own hearts. Kenniontie looks down at her as if to say something, but Gaianniana emerges from the orchard asking what has kept her so long. Tsiatekenha stands and beckons for Eunice to come with him and Gaianniana to pick strawberries, but the rest of the day has a shadow over it. She cannot keep her mind on picking the berries that they have been mashing for days to make a sweet drink for the Strawberry Festival that ushers in the summer.

When Eunice returns to the longhouse toward evening, Kenniontie looks at her intently. "Maybe the priest has spoken to you?" she asks, studying Eunice closely for any change in her manner.

"No," replies Eunice. "Gaianniana and I picked strawberries, and Tsiatekenha made tops with us until some boys began to tease us with their bows." Kenniontie looks relieved.

"Daughter, Achiendase will come to see you soon. He will take you to the mission for a visit." Kenniontie's intent look makes Eunice uneasy. Why should she make so much of a visit to the mission? Eunice searches her face. Will Achiendase take her to Onnontio, the French governor? Eunice has heard of children being bought by the French and sold back to their families. Perhaps it is her turn.

That night she imagines her family scattered through the vast woods, looking at the same crescent moon. Could her father come here with the governor? For the first time, she imagines her family at Kahnawake. She sleeps with her silver cup in her hand.

CHAPTER 9

The next morning, Kenniontie runs a carved wooden comb through Eunice's hair, taking special care to smooth it with oil, attaching pretty feathers and beads for decoration. She even paints red spots, usually reserved for grown women on special occasions, high on Eunice's cheekbones. Outside the longhouse, Achiendase greets Kenniontie and her brother Onwekowa before bending to take Eunice's hand. But Onwekowa insists that he sit and pass the ceremonial pipe, as people are expected to do before business of any importance. Again, all Eunice knows with any certainty is that the governor, Onnontio, seems to want to see her and that Kenniontie is concerned about it. He must be very powerful.

When they have finished passing the pipe, Achiendase takes Eunice by the hand to take her to the mission. Kenniontie strokes her hair, tips her face up, and plants a firm kiss on Eunice's freshly painted cheek. "Don't worry," she says. "Atironta and I will be waiting for you outside. We'll be right behind you."

Achiendase is quiet at first. Eunice wants to ask him what is happening, but at the same time, she is afraid of the answer. It is as if a spell has taken hold of her. But as they reach the woods Achiendase speaks to her in English.

"Asientie, Kenniontie—they are kind?" he asks.

Eunice only nods.

"You have friends at Kahnawake." This is a statement and it is true, but she wonders why he is saying it. "The children here are happy. The Kahnawake people are kind." It is as if he had studied how to say these words. There is a pause. She hears the song of a wood thrush disappearing in the dappled woods.

"You will see the Reverend Williams," Achiendase tells her, giving her hand a squeeze. Eunice looks up at him in confusion and amazement. Achiendase hurries on before she can ask if she is going home. "But your father is a . . ." He seems to search for a word. ". . . a prisoner. He must return to Quebec with the priest who has brought him here."

They come out of the woods into Achiendase's settlement. Eunice can hardly take it in. "He is in the mission house," says Achiendase. "You will have some time with him, but he is not free to take you with him."

Eunice can't help but register the look of astonishment on her father's face when she enters the mission house. She herself has given no thought to her transformation over the past few months, but sees it reflected in her father's eyes. The mission house is dark, and immediately she wishes that they could meet outside in the sunshine as people usually do in the summer. And there is a wrinkle gathering on her father's brow. His disapproval is not entirely banished from his eyes as he crosses the room and bends down to take her in his arms. It makes her shrink a little. He smells strange, and she finds herself watching the swelling of his Adam's apple as he swallows repeatedly before speaking. Holding her away from him after their embrace, his mouth tightens.

"'Tis a long time that I have looked for this moment," he says. "God is merciful. We must give thanks for the mercy He has shown us. Have you been able to keep in mind your prayers, Eunice?"

She looks searchingly at her father. What mercy? God was merciful to the Reverend. But her mother, John, Jerusha, and Parthena are dead. And prayers? He would not like the ones she has been saying. But what of her brothers and sister?

"Stephen?" she asks hopefully. Perhaps there *is* some mercy.

"Eunice, have you kept your prayers in mind? Let us first pray." Why doesn't he answer her? But she nods as the Reverend begins the Lord's Prayer. Indeed, the English prayer comes right back to her as they recite it, though her mind remains numbed with questions.

Satisfied with the prayer, the Reverend begins to speak with cautious, measured tones.

"Your sister has been redeemed from the French and is on her way to Boston even now. You too will be redeemed, Eunice. Samuel and Warham are with French families," her father continues. "They get on well enough, though I am anxious for the welfare of their souls. The priests are ever at them with their devilish beliefs. Samuel, in particular, seems beguiled by the Catholic ways. Hold fast to your faith, Eunice. I pray we shall all soon be redeemed."

But will they? Eunice is confused. First he sounded certain they would be redeemed, but now he is praying for it.

Her father seems to sense her confusion and goes on. "And you, Eunice? They will not let you go with me now, any more than they will let me return to Massachusetts. We must bear ourselves with patience. I see that you remember your prayers. But there must be much you would repent of among these heathen. Beware of the Jesuit who brought you to me. These Jesuits, the Catholic priests, are full of wiles and clever traps. Take care for your soul and tell me all that has befallen you. The Lord tests us mightily, but he will also show us His grace."

Eunice has the curious sensation that she alone of her family is somehow in disgrace. A fist is forming in her throat. She is burning in her father's gaze as she stands in her loose beaded tunic with its beautiful tree of peace. She reads in her father's eyes that her dress sets her apart from her redeemed siblings, who have been bought from other tribes by the French. She cannot understand whether her father will come back for her soon or not. And he has not told her about Stephen.

"Where is my brother Stephen?" she asks again.

"Stephen is with another group of savages, the Abenaki. I have not laid eyes upon him, but am assured that he is well. God willing we shall all soon be redeemed and reunited. Our good neighbors work for our release. Eunice, again I say, you must have much to repent of living among savages and Jesuits as you do. You must try to tell me of your struggles that your soul may be cleansed of heathen influence. You must repent of the Devil's influence so that we may pray together as good Christians before I go. I will not leave this bondage without you."

Is the Devil's influence in the Latin prayers? In the pictures? She casts about for her father's meaning, for clearly he demands an answer.

"They make me say some prayers in Latin," she says haltingly, pausing for a minute as she searches for words. "Joanna Kellogg says they cannot do us harm, for we know nothing of their meaning."

"It is the Devil's work, Jesuitry, that she should say this,

Eunice." His tone is even but he seems to bite off each word, "And you must tell Joanna this for the sake of her soul too. These Jesuits are full of ingenious argument. The Lord is testing us sorely and we must daily repent of our wickedness. One may not live unsullied among the heathen. Do you repent of the Latin prayers? Is there aught else that you would tell me?"

Again Eunice feels compelled to search for something. Neither Achiendase nor the Kahnawake speak of sin. She thinks of their dancing the night before and the sweetness of a strawberry drink passed among them. But there is nothing sinful in dancing or good food. Even the most devout Puritan saints dance and eat sweet cakes at celebrations. What can she tell her father?

"There is a picture in the mission of a saint who looks like Mother. I look at it when we pray," she says.

The look of pain and outrage on the Reverend's face is a rebuke in itself. "Your mother is in Heaven," he says sharply. "You must not pray to devilish idols. We will pray for your salvation. I see that you are sorely tested, Eunice."

Achiendase returns while Eunice and her father are praying. He waits for the prayer to end before crossing the room. Eunice watches her father rise from his chair. "Let me go with you." The words seem to escape without her thinking them.

When he bends to kiss her, she wants to cling to him, but he says quickly, "You must be strong. I will come back for you." Achiendase leads him out by a door she has never noticed before as Atironta steps into the room through the door she knows.

When Eunice emerges from the mission with Atironta, the sun is flaming behind a green filigree of summer leaves to the west of the stockade. As soon as her eyes adjust to the brightness, a wave of tears washes over her at the sight of Kenniontie.

• • •

During the next week, Kenniontie and the younger women keep Eunice busy with all kinds of activities. Today's is the most exciting: They are headed toward the island of Montreal. Their canoe shoots forward as the rapids grab it. Kenniontie and Sientiesie ply their paddles; the white water churns and spits; foam flies. The thrust of the canoe as it rides over the tumult of waters is thrilling. Eunice, with Ohnwatsihon low in the boat before her, cannot imagine that the powerful water will do anything but hurl them toward the city. It is a large canoe, and Eunice and Ohnwatsihon are surrounded by the goods she has helped the women pack for a day of trading and sightseeing.

"A'onote!" When they get clear of the rapids, Kenniontie motions her to come up to the bow. Sientiesie takes Ohnwatsihon, and Eunice climbs forward, carefully balancing the rocking boat with her feet the way Kenniontie has shown her, so she can sit in front of Kenniontie and practice paddling.

When they enter the flats, the sun glances off the silver wrinkles on the surface. It looks like the cloak of sunlight the great mother Ataensic wore when she fell to earth, Eunice thinks, remembering a story the old woman Asientie, mother to Kenniontie and her brothers, has told her. She likes to think of the sky woman, undefeated in death, who continues to light the world. Though she struggles to understand them, the stories Asientie tells her remind her of Parthena's tales.

Eunice checks her grip, trying to match her motions to Kenniontie's just behind her. Paddling in the bow gives her dominion over the scene that unfurls ahead of them. In the silky shallows, the folded shape of a heron opens out into flight as it detaches itself from a congregation of assorted wading birds. Gulls skim the river. Ducks and geese bob in assorted groups. A kingfisher dives right next to the canoe. Beyond them, a colorful flotilla of canoes and French bateaux spans the river's width, most piled high with furs or bright fabrics. Eunice has helped Kenniontie and Sientiesie load their canoe not only with these but with wampum made over the winter and baskets of the strawberries she has gathered from the woods and fields with Gaianniana, since the corn and beans have not come in yet. Just west of the wall that surrounds the town, there are lines of canoes and bateaux pulled up on the riverbank, where a bazaar has been set up and people move among piles of trade goods.

A chorus of shouts passes among the boats, and suddenly Kenniontie points and shouts herself.

"A'onote, Look ahead! A whale has come to greet you! I have not seen one so far up river before! Beautiful." Looking to the deeper channel where Kenniontie points, Eunice sees only a moving expanse of what looks like slick white clay before the water closes over it.

Eunice doesn't watch for long because her attention is drawn to the town that rises on the island ahead, shimmering in the sun. There are more buildings than she has ever seen and a long wall of stone. The buildings come almost down to the shore, where the stone wall begins, and their roofs gleam in the intense, misty light.

"Can we see *la horloge* from here?" she asks as they draw nearer to the shore. Ever since Joanna Kellogg told her about the clock she has had the idea that because it is so large the clock will mark the days and months of the year, that her time in Kahnawake will be recorded, and she will see it there made real.

"Not from here," replies Kenniontie. "It is on the far side of town."

The shore itself is alive with bustling bodies. Eunice runs her fingers over the wampum she has stitched and wonders what she will trade it for.

"Look up!" says Sientiesie, lifting her arm to gesture as they pull the canoe up onto the shore. She is pointing to the carved figure of a woman beckoning from a roof. "Our Lady of Bon Secours, to protect travelers on the river. She is pretty, *kadon*!"

Kenniontie lifts Ohnwatsihon into her arms, and they leave Sientiesie with the canoe while they head into the town to get a treat Kenniontie has promised them.

It seems to Eunice that the whole world must come together in Montreal. There are people of all kinds in various states of dress and undress. French men and women in rich brocades and laces, Indian men in breech clouts and some in fancy dress, traders dressed in beaver hats and skins, some poor, some rich, some beautifully dressed and some ragged and dirty as if in from a long sojourn in the wilderness. She looks down at the beautiful beadwork on her tunic as a woman in a dress of rose brocade stops to look at her for a moment. Kenniontie tightens her grip on her shoulder. She wonders if the woman can tell she is not a Kahnawake girl. Maybe she wanted to bargain for her the way French people traded for Samuel, Esther, and Warham. And her father too, she suddenly realizes. The strangeness of her meeting with him washes over her again.

All around her there are people hawking goods. And there are shops on the streets leading up from the river. Bakeries, butchers, spirit shops, candle makers. All with painted signs or carvings to show what they sell. The confusion of sounds, smells, colors is like nothing she has known before. They stop to buy some cakes from a Frenchwoman carrying a tray on the street, and Eunice exchanges a small piece of wampum for the treat. It melts in her mouth, and for a moment she thinks of Parthena and Deerfield. But there is so much going on around her that she cannot hold a thought for long. She is jostled by a passerby on the street, takes Onhwatsihon's hand as Kenniontie puts him down, and when she looks up she is bewildered to see her father coming toward her. She thought he had been taken back to Quebec. She sees no master with him.

The Reverend looks equally startled, but embarrassed too. Kenniontie stops, polite but guarded, one hand on Eunice's shoulder, to allow her father to speak. She keeps her hand firmly on Eunice's shoulder.

"*Kannonhoeron*," Kenniontie greets him before Eunice can say anything, and her father returns the greeting in English and turns to Eunice.

"It pains me to see you like this, Eunice. You must understand that I am helpless to take you from your mistress." Eunice regards him wordlessly. "I am working as I can to secure your release and I pray for you every hour of the day. Do not forget your prayers, Eunice. Our best comfort is in God."

She doesn't know what to say to her father. He seems to have grown stranger and stiffer since their last meeting. And yet, he seems to her as free as anyone on the street. What is it she should pray for? Kenniontie squeezes her shoulder, urging her to speak.

"I will pray, Father," Eunice replies, echoing his words, but she can think of nothing else and looks to Kenniontie for help.

The Reverend is momentarily distracted by a woman dressed in bright blue silk, her powdered hair piled impossibly high on her head, hurrying down the busy street toward the harbor.

"God go with you, Eunice. I will return to redeem you," he

tells her, but as he begins to reach out, Kenniontie steps between them with a worried look and he backs away a step.

Eunice's eyes go hard. No, you will not, she thinks.

Ohnwatsihon tugs at her hand. "*Oghniyawenhonh?*" he asks, but Eunice doesn't know what is happening, except that her father is walking away.

Kenniontie squeezes Eunice's hand, and leads them to the Sulpician Monastery, a great stone building whose size alone is astonishing to Eunice, who once thought their little meetinghouse in Deerfield was very large. The building looks forbidding, sitting there on the northern wall of the city, cold-looking even on a summer's day. Eunice cranes her neck to see the great square clock face on the tower Joanna told her about, and watches its long wrought-iron arrow cover a span of time marked by letters that tell her nothing.

CHAPTER 10

Eunice tosses in her closeted bed. She shivers and she is burning up. She kicks off the blankets and furs that cover her, then sits up in her sleep searching for them. Tsihon anxiously settles and resettles, trying to keep her warm. There is a high, whining sound working its way into her dreams. Her sister, Esther, is at the spinning wheel. She hears the steady rhythmic knocking sound of the treadle, the wheel's high singing, the spindle whirling like a top. Esther steps back and forward again in a graceful dance with the wheel as she holds high the twisting, quivering strands of flax. Her hands move high and low tossing the delicate strands, silvery as a spider's web in the moonlight. But doesn't Esther need help? Eunice is suddenly in a panic. It is *she* who should be spinning. Why can't she get to Esther? Stumbling out of the sleeping closet, Eunice finds herself standing dazed and shivering by the guttering hearth fire. Tsihon follows, whining and nudging her hand with her cold nose. As she sinks down by the fire, she feels a quivering inside, and her eyes feel hot and dry. It hardly matters where she is. She feels too strange to notice. She only wants her mother. She puts her head down on the cool floor mat. The vines carved into a swirling floral design on the wooden chest nearby seem to be slithering like snakes through the dark flowers. Closing her eyes, she sees a burst of small bright lights behind her eyelids. Somewhere between sleep and waking she cries out, "*Oghniyawenhonh*? What is happening?"

A moment later Kenniontie, Atironta, and Asientie are all by her side. Kenniontie is wrapping blankets around her and Atironta adds wood to the fire. She sees Kenniontie and Asientie peering anxiously into her face as the fire leaps up. Her face feels hot, and she is trembling.

"It is the scarlet fever. Her skin feels rough, and she is burning hot," Kenniontie tells them. "We must bathe her."

Eunice's head is pounding. The pounding picks up and then eases as Kenniontie bathes her face and shoulders in cool water, but she begins shivering violently now, her teeth almost chattering.

"Will you bring the bundle that hangs next to the red wampum, sister? She is burning with fever." Eunice sees that Sientiesie has crept out of her closet on the other side of the hearth and stands looking anxiously at them across the fire. She nods and gets the quilled skin bag and brings it to Kenniontie.

"Thank you, sister. Do you think you might take Ohnwatsihon to the hunting camp?" Kenniontie asks. "Maybe you can stay there with his father's people for a time. They have not seen much of Ohnwatsihon since his father was killed last fall." She has already begun mixing a poultice from the medicine bag.

Eunice hears their talk dimly, and, in spite of her wooziness and the burning in her throat, understands enough. She tries to speak, but the words won't come. She feels ashamed that her sickness is driving Sientiesie and Ohnwatsihon from the house. What if

Ohnwatsihon gets sick and dies? Will they think that she has brought it on him? Will they hate her for it? Eunice leans against Atironta while Kenniontie bathes her face and chest, softly singing some words of which Eunice can only catch the refrain, "*Nihaweh-kowa*, great thanks," a refrain that echoes the songs of the strawberry festival. She looks up at Kenniontie's intent black eyes in the firelight. "*Nihawehkowa*," she manages to rasp, then turns her head toward Atironta. "*Nihawehkowa*."

Silent tears tickle her cheeks. She is so grateful to be taken care of, encircled so. She wants to apologize to Sientiesie for endangering Ohnwatsihon, but she is too tired to find the words. The poultice that Kenniontie applies is soothing, and her shivering quiets as she is wrapped in a blanket. She closes her eyes briefly, then gazes up at the flickering rafters, hearing once more the high singing sound that came into her dream and woke her. Looking up at Atironta, she points to the arched ceiling and asks him about the sound. And he tells her a story about the wind in a singsong voice that lulls her to sleep before he finishes. It is the story of Ataensic, the Sky Woman, who brought beans, corn, and squash down to the earth, and how the west wind gave her daughter twin boys, who competed at all kinds of games and struggles and made a balance between good and evil in the world.

"Healing comes out of sickness," Atironta tells her.

Falling back to sleep, she dreams of Sky Woman and her daughter, and the fighting twins. But the twins become Stephen and Samuel racing on the parade grounds in Deerfield, Sky Woman's cloak of sunlight turns blue, and she sees her mother shaking its folds so they fall smoothly before going out the door in Deerfield. This image gets all mixed up with the heavenly mother in the painting in the mission. Sometimes she thinks she is in Deerfield, sometimes in the high place under the cedars that Gaianniana showed her. But she keeps hearing Esther at her spinning wheel and thinking she must go to her. Eunice can't tell how long she hovers between sleep and waking, sickness and health, but it seems like many days.

There are always voices around her, snatches of conversation that come and go and become part of her dreams. There is talk of the Society of the Mystic Animals and of the otter, a spirit helper that they call on because it moves between two worlds. There is also talk of the False Face Society that might release her from her dreams. She hears her name, "A'onote, A'onote, A'onote," in Kenniontie's, Asientie's, Atironta's, even Achiendase's voice.

She is so weak, at first she hardly notices when the dancers begin filtering into the house. The singing and drumming goes on for some time, but this she has heard before. It is when she sees the red and black masks appearing out of the shadows around her with their wild black hair and twisted faces that she becomes alarmed. Their voices are strong and true, but the faces are terrible. Two have spoonlike mouths that protrude from their devilish masks. These two close in on the fire and begin blowing ashes all around while the other two continue to dance and sing, advancing and then backing away from the flying ashes in mock fear. Soon there are embers flying around the hearth like a thousand fireflies, and the singing grows louder and higher. She looks for Atironta and Kenniontie, but they are nowhere in sight. There are dancers behind the masks, but they might also be devils. She is too frail to care. She simply watches with fascination as, in turn, each mask sings to her, one voice sweeter than the next, and the two who blew the ashes lay small medicine bundles at her head and feet before withdrawing, still singing with a deep resonant humming as they leave.

She falls into a deep sleep, like diving into a black pool. She sees a turtle dive down into the pond and resurface with an island on its back. Then a girl she doesn't recognize cries *"Jathondek! Listen!"* And there is a deep, rumbling chant that grows louder and louder. All around the pond are bears, buffalos, otters, and eagles that spread and flap their wings under the arching sky. The whole Society of Mystic Animals has surrounded the pond, chanting in a strange tongue, and their shapes are reflected in the smooth, glassy surface of the pond. She plunges and surfaces, becomes one with the black water. Something glimmers on the bottom and she dives for it, a small smooth stone, which she places in her mouth. I am otter, she says, as she surfaces and rolls onto her back to see the dome of the sky above her. I am A'onote. *Enyoriwadatye.* It will go on.

· · ·

When A'onote awakens, Kenniontie, Asientie, and Atironta are by her side. Tsihon, who has stayed by her side throughout her illness, nudges her with her nose. Sientiesie has returned, quiet and serious with her son in her arms, and sits down beside them. The corn pudding cooking on the hearth smells enticing. For the first time in many days A'onote is hungry.

"*Oghniyawenhonh?*" she asks, looking at the family surrounding her.

"You are back with us," answers Kenniontie. "The False Face Society has danced for you. They must have seemed frightening, but they helped you. And you have been one with the otter, who lives in two worlds. I heard you say it in your dream. One day you will join the Otter Society. You have a spirit helper already now. You will see how she will help you when you need her. Even more than Tsihon," she adds. "Now you must eat and rest."

. . .

A'onote hears more about this from Kenniontie the next day.

"We must give thanks and keep you well. 'She Who Is Planted with Us.' That is the meaning of your name, A'onote. You are planted deep in our hearts. Soon, when the corn comes in, we will hold a ceremony during the Green Corn Festival to confirm your name and your place among us, and this will be set in the record with a fine strip of wampum. As long as you live, no one else will have this name. It will let all the people know that you are now *Keniahten*, a person of the Turtle Clan, which Asientie and I belong to. This is the first and most powerful clan among us, because it is the Turtle on whose back the earth rests, as our stories tell you. You will grow up to be *royaneh*, a woman who holds much power, a leader in the Women's Council, and a healer. In all this, you will follow the women of our lineage."

"And Atironta? Is he of the Turtle Clan?"

"Atironta is *Akotthaghyonnighshon*, of the Wolf Clan, like Gaianniana and her mother. That is the second clan. As children our people are all—girls and boys alike—taken into the clan of our mothers, who plant the fields, nourish us, and own our lands and homes. Our mothers determine our roles among the people, and we inherit from them. The Canienga people have the Turtle, Wolf, and Bear clans. To be of the Bear Clan is *Akskerewake*. Each of these clans has its own power, and each has members in all the five nations of the Great Peace, the Haudenosaunee League, which includes the Canienga, Onondaga, Seneca, Oneida, and Cayuga nations."

A'onote remembers Kenniontie telling her about these nations, the People of the Longhouse, of the Great Peace. She thinks her father used to talk about them too, but she can't remember why.

Kenniontie continues, "We can marry people of our own tribe, but we do not marry people of our own clan. Atironta is a peace chief, more powerful than the war chiefs, and chosen by the Women's Council to lead. When the Great Peace was established, generations before the Europeans came, the founders of the Haudenosaunee League wanted the women's voices and those of the peace chiefs like Atironta to be stronger than the voices for war. It is hard now, with the English and French, but most of the time we have kept the peace among ourselves."

"Atironta went to fight with the French, when he brought me from Deerfield."

"Yes. That was what we call a Mourning War. The Women's Council proclaims it only when we have lost too many of our people to war or sickness. A few years ago, Atironta and I lost our daughter, Gannestenawi, to smallpox. It's part of the Great Peace to adopt new children to fill the seats of the people we have lost, instead of taking revenge by killing whole villages. This is why we adopt the people we take. We don't put them in prisons the way the English do."

"Do the French put people in prisons?" asks A'onote. Her father seemed perfectly free when she saw him.

"Sometimes, but not so often. They adopt people, too, just as as we are adopting you."

"Until my father returns," A'onote says, but Kenniontie goes on.

"You are tired now. You will learn more before the corn comes in. Now rest."

A'onote is left to turn all this over in her mind. Kenniontie did not say if her father would come back. She is still not sure what it means to be adopted. Can her father take her back if she is adopted? It occurs to her that there are things she will miss when he comes. She thinks of him disappearing into the crowded streets of Montreal. He had no master with him. Surely he can come back for her. Does he want to? She wonders if he thinks she has become a devil. A devil Maqua, he might say, now that she is about to join the Turtle Clan and be adopted as one of their own by the Kahnawake people and the larger nation of the Haudenosaunee.

The following day, A'onote is allowed a visitor. Gaianniana arrives as Kenniontie returns to work in the fields and Asientie sets off for a meeting of the Otter Society, the healing society made up only of women. Gaianniana seems glad to see A'onote and greets Tsihon affectionately with a bit of pemmican.

"Let's go outside," A'onote suggests before Gaianniana can settle herself.

"Asientie says you have to stay out of the light for a few more days. You have been very sick." Gaianniana pauses. "I am glad you are better. I was afraid you would die like my cousin Gannestenawi. I miss her."

"What was she like?"

"She was a little older than you, like I am." This does not satisfy A'onote's curiosity, but she has been told that it is not good to speak of the dead. "Your people and the French and Dutch brought awful sicknesses to us. We never had them before. Whole villages used to die. Asientie can tell you. Her first family, a husband and a little boy, died of smallpox. Most of her village died, and she nearly died herself." Gaianniana gestures toward her face. "That is why her face is pockmarked."

A'onote raises her hand to her own face.

"You have no marks," Gaianniana reassures her. "The scarlet fever doesn't do that. Kateri Tekakwitha, the Kahnawake saint in the mission painting, had the smallpox like Asientie did, years before she came to Kahnawake. Asientie knew her. She became a great healer and led a group of holy women who followed the priests. Asientie is a healer but not like Kateri. Asientie believes in old ways."

"That is why she doesn't go to the mission?"

"She is friendly with Achiendase, but she never goes into the mission. Sometimes she goes to the chapel our people built here on our own land but only for very special occasions," says Gaianniana. Then suddenly she blurts out, "I didn't want you here when you came. I didn't like to think of you taking Gannestenawi's place. I missed her so much. I still think I see her sometimes, like a shadow in the corner of my eye. If I'm sleepy I might think I see her at the edge of the bonfire. And then I know I am wrong. She was the sister of my heart."

"I am taking her place?" The thought that she is to replace someone is strange and frightening, though now she understands that this is what Kenniontie meant when she said children were adopted in the seat of those who had been lost, and she sees that Gaianniana has been unhappy about her taking Gannestenawi's place. "Ok'e," she says cautiously. "But I will not be staying here."

Gaianniana looks surprised. "I think you will stay," she answers. "That is why Atironta brought you. This is the reason for the Mourning War that the Women's Council called for. One day you and I will sit on the Women's Council together. I don't think the English women have such a thing. They say the English women don't even own their houses and fields."

"That isn't true," says A'onote.

But she realizes she doesn't know.

• • •

All the time A'onote was recovering from scarlet fever, the blueberries were ripening and the women were beginning to dry them for pemmican. Now that she is strong again, she has been picking berries with Gaianniana, and today Joanna is coming along to a spot that Gaianniana says will still be full of berries. It is almost time for the Green Corn Festival.

"Joanna!" Looking over at Gaianniana, A'onote corrects herself and uses Joanna's Canienga name. "Gentiyo, I'm glad to see you! Gaianniana says there is a place to swim near the blueberries. She is going to show us how!"

"I've been swimming for weeks," says Joanna. "But then, I wasn't sick like you were. Everyone was so frightened of losing you. Achiendase gave me a long string of beads. *Rosaire*, they are called. Each bead stands for a prayer, and I used them to pray for you."

"You know," says Gaianniana as they head out of the gate in the stockade, "we have a visitor at our house, my older cousin Arosen. He has come from our Canienga people to the south, at Canajoharie Castle, in English territory. He is your age, Gentiyo. Wolf Clan like me. I like him. He knows some of the places you and A'onote must know, I think. You can both meet him at the festival."

They chatter on until they reach the place where the blueberries grow. A'onote is happy to have Joanna with them. It is comforting to have someone else who has come so far. And she is curious about this boy who knows something of her country.

The blueberries grow along the edge of a big pool in the river. When they finish picking, they sit on a broad, flat rock warmed by the sun. Gaianniana sits down and pulls her shift over her head, and Joanna follows. A'onote hesitates for a moment, then follows suit. She looks at Joanna and Gaianniana lifting their feet in the shallow water, slowly and carefully like wading birds, sinewy and brown in the lacy sunlight. With a look over her shoulder and a dip of her legs, Joanna propels herself into the obsidian pool and glides across it, her arms reaching in smooth strokes, her kicking feet sending sparkling crystals leaping in the sunlight. Her movements are so sure and swift that A'onote knows that the she will not sink, knows it with a shiver of excitement and fear. Suddenly, Eunice remembers trading tales with Mary Brooks one gray afternoon. "My mother says people think that witches will not sink. 'Tis how one knows them." Mary's family had come from Salem, where they held the witch trials. "My mother said people might say that anyone they didn't like was a witch. And they hanged the witches while people watched." She had learned a great many things from Mary. Now it seems to be Joanna and Gaianniana she learns from.

A'onote ventures knee deep in the water. The rock beneath her feet is slimy with moss and she moves slowly. Water bugs glide around her leaving delicate v-shaped tracks on the water's surface. There are speckled trout and baby salmon hovering beneath rock ledges. Joanna is swimming back toward her, sleek as an otter, beckoning. A'onote takes another step, slips on a sudden incline, and loses her footing on the mossy rock. Even as the frigid water closes over her, she feels clear-headed. When she begins to struggle, Gaianniana is at her side, hooking an arm under her own, reaching up toward her chin and towing her across the pool like a water bug. She gains a stumbling foothold on the sandy bottom at the far side. The three girls throw themselves wordlessly on the sandy spit, hunching their shivering bodies. A'onote is numb and her chilly brain tingles with energy. Joanna laughs, "You are too quick. Wait for us to teach you, *kadon.*"

By the time they gather up their baskets of blueberries, A'onote has begun to swim a little, cupping her hands and paddling like Tsihon. No one ever swam in Deerfield. She wants to come to this spot and swim every day. But tomorrow begins the Green Corn Festival, where she and Joanna will officially be given their new names and adopted into their separate families and clans.

"Don't worry," says Joanna when Gaianniana wanders off on her own. "I have heard that people are adopted by the Kahnawake and still go home. It doesn't mean you will have to stay if your father comes. I'm sure it's different if there is someone to take you home." She pauses a minute and laughs. "I don't think I could make myself put my old clothes on. Do you remember how the bone stays in our dresses hurt when we bent or sat down? No wonder our mothers didn't seem very happy."

A'onote remembers her conversation with Gaianniana. "Do our houses belong to our mothers?" she asks. The fields could not have belonged to them, since they rarely went into them she thinks, but the houses could.

"No," answers Joanna. "I never thought about it then, but nothing belonged to our mothers. I think I might be glad to stay here and become a member of the Women's Council someday. I don't think being adopted is a bad thing. It means you can belong to two worlds." Like the otter, thinks A'onote.

CHAPTER 11

The next day, the village is alive again with the sound of flutes, drums, and the dry rattle of the gourds for the Green Corn Festival. Gaianniana has explained that the people will give thanks to the Life Supporters and dance and feast for days. The babies born since the Midwinter Festival will be named; and Eunice, Joanna, and other Deerfield children scattered among the Kahnawake people will take their new names and be adopted into their families in separate clan ceremonies. She reminds herself of Joanna's new name, Gentiyo, meaning Beautiful Plain. A'onote takes out the pretty, beaded, knee-high moccasins Kenniontie made for her to wear for the ceremony, admiring the fancy beadwork as she slips them on. Kenniontie has oiled her hair and woven ribbons into it earlier in the day. And A'onote's face has been painted again as it was in the wilderness, this time to ready her for her adoption ceremony.

As A'onote approaches the adoption circle with Asientie, she is surprised by loud wailing, as if the entire assembly were in mourning. She sees Kenniontie and Atironta waiting for her in the center of the circle. Gaianniana's father, Onwekowa, is there too with his younger brother, Tsiatekenha, to represent the Turtle Clan. Gaianniana and her mother and many others, some whom A'onote doesn't recognize, are ranged around the circle representing the Wolf Clan. The wailing rises and falls with the drumbeats.

"A'onote," Asientie whispers, before leading her into the center of the circle, "do not be worried by the wailing. We must wail for Gannestenawi's spirit, which has to be sent off once more, before we can adopt you in her seat. It will turn to celebration very quickly, since she has gone to the world she now belongs in."

The wailing subsides, and Onwekowa steps forward to speak.

"Here are Kenniontie and Atironta and their daughter A'onote, who will henceforth be of the Turtle Clan. This child is adopted in Gannestenawi's honored seat. We have mourned her once more, and her spirit now belongs to the sky world. This life on the Turtle's back belongs only to you, A'onote. One day you will be called Gannestenawi, and you will still be planted in our hearts. You will have many names and nothing will be lost." He goes on for a while, and for A'onote, it is a little like being in the meetinghouse or the mission: after some time, she no longer hears the words. But they also make her feel that she is important and welcome. Finally, On-wekowa, A'onote's uncle now, repeats her name twice, takes her hand, and leads her around the circle singing a song about the Great Peace she is now a part of, represented by the splendid tree on her tunic. As he sings, Atironta's people, including Gaianniana and an older boy who stands beside her, chant the traditional chant, "*Hyenh, hyenh, hyenh*," until the song is ended, and all are allowed to come forward and welcome her.

Gaianniana takes her by the hand and gestures to the tall boy beside her. "This is my cousin Arosen from the south," she says.

"Welcome, A'onote."

"*Niyawehkowa*," she answers. Arosen is wearing a fine quill-work shirt with two stripes of yellow beads for the ceremony. She notices a white scar on his cheekbone, a fine, thin line cut by something sharp.

"We cannot dance with the grown-ups, but there is a children's dance nearby," says Gaianniana as they cross the Kahnawake village.

When they join the children, A'onote races toward Joanna. No, Gentiyo, she thinks, and stops, amazed. There with Gentiyo stands her brother, Joseph Kellogg. His hair is almost white from the sun, but his skin and eyes are brown like Gentiyo's.

"Eunice!" he exclaims. "My sister told me you were here."

"A'onote," says Joanna, brimming with happiness. "Joseph arrived here last night. He is alive. I have two families." A'onote's eyes fill with tears at the sight of him. It is almost as if one of her own brothers has arrived.

Joseph has been with the Huron, a tribe friendly with the Canienga, though not a member of the Five Nations. He and his Huron master remain for a few weeks before returning to their travels. In fact, many of the people who gathered at Kahnawake in the summer begin to disperse, visitors returning to their own villages to help out with the harvest or heading out to trade in distant territories. Joseph leaves without a word. She hears he has left from Gentiyo. Soon after this, Arosen comes to visit her family and say good-bye. He gives her a piece of flint that looks like a turtle. The flint is smooth and black with sharp edges along the side of the turtle shell. It is just about the size of her open palm.

"Because you are of the Turtle Clan and one of the People of the Flint," he says. "Keep it with you. It is good for all kinds of little jobs."

She is surprised that this older boy would think to make something for her, but these small kindnesses seem to be the rule in this new world.

PART III

THE DOOR IN THE COUNTRY
OCTOBER 1705–FEBRUARY 1708

CHAPTER 12

The moon hangs round and gold and seems larger than it has ever been before. Nine years old now, A'onote has lived a year and a half among the Kahnawake people, and the fall Harvest Festival has come a second time. She has learned to use her flint turtle for many things—cutting threads, smoothing sticks for roasting small game, even softening hides brought back from the hunting camps. She has tucked her silver cup, now blue-black with tarnish, into a special medicine pouch she keeps in Asientie's carved trunk.

Tonight, the fire in the square outside the central longhouse seems hotter and wilder than any fire has ever been. There is a nip in the air. A'onote once again has a fur vest over her tunic, the fur turned inward. Bowls of popped corn are being passed, light and airy white, sprung like magic from the parched kernel. People move around the fire like shadows, but many are familiar now. The moon comes and goes, waxes and wanes. It is cold, then warm, then cold again. Gentiyo is sometimes in the village, sometimes not. The image of her mother grows strong and fades again. Her father and siblings live or die; she cannot know.

During the past week, Atironta and Kenniontie have been up at one of the hunting camps in the mountains, where he will hunt deer, wild turkey, and quail, and she will collect medicines and help stretch the deerskins and preserve the meat he brings in. When A'onote asked if she could go with them, Kenniontie told her that they would be much too busy and that she was not yet old enough to be helpful. Atironta promised that they would not be long. Now A'onote leans her head on Sientiesie's shoulder while Ohnwatsihon sleeps in his mother's lap. A'onote looks up and sees shadows dancing on Sientiesie's cheek as she talks quietly to a woman next to her.

"Kenniontie would not see her," she tells the woman. "She refuses all offers to trade her for one of our people."

"Who did Kenniontie refuse to see?" A'onote, who has almost fallen asleep, sits up abruptly. "Did my father come for me?"

Sientiesie looks down at her, surprised. "No," she answers. "It was Onnontio's wife from Montreal. The Reverend Williams cannot redeem you. He is not free himself. You are better here with us, A'onote. You are in our hearts."

A'onote reaches her hand into a bowl as it is passed and takes a handful of the popped kernels. Kenniontie would not even see the French governor's wife. How could she refuse someone so important?

The air has a bite to it. Winter is not far off. Piles of corn lie all around them, for they have been husking and braiding it to prepare winter stores and seed for the spring. In Deerfield, they would have been doing many of the same things, but instead of the storytelling that goes on all winter here, her father would be reading to them from the Bible every night. A'onote pulls a blanket around her shoulders and leans over to tuck another around Ohnwatsihon on Sientiesie's lap. She looks up at Sientiesie's quiet face. For some reason her seriousness reminds A'onote of Joanna looking into a much smaller fire when the girls were left together on their way to Canada, *to Kahnawake*, she says under her breath, and Sientiesie looks down at her questioningly and asks if she is cold. No, not cold, she wants to say, I am not cold, but I am strange. She doesn't know how else to describe the feeling that she has been under this spectacular moon forever and yet is forever separated from her home.

It is late when Sientiesie gathers up Ohnwatsihon and takes a sleepy A'onote by the hand. The moon is resting on the horizon before dipping away, so close that a person might walk to it, thinks A'onote.

"Atironta and Kenniontie will return soon," says Sientiesie. "Don't worry. They didn't think it was safe to take you with them now." Ohnwatsihon straightens and lifts his head from Sientiesie's shoulder. He looks around for a moment before looking up at his mother and settling back to sleep. "There is a truce in the war between the French and the English, but there have been a few attacks on our people here and there. Kenniontie and Atironta know how to stay safe, but they might meet up with anyone on their trip."

A'onote wonders sleepily what it means that they might meet anyone. She looks ahead at the moon balancing so expertly on the horizon and wishes she could have gone with them. What if Kenniontie and Atironta returned with her family? It is suddenly easy to imagine Stephen, Warham, and John walking back from the fire to the longhouse. No, not John. He is in Heaven with mother and Parthena and the baby. But the others could be here. She remembers the four of them huddled in the lean-to they built, and she can almost hear the sound of John's voice, how it piped unlike the other's voices. Suddenly she hears it cut through the cold and dark as she lies in her bed in Deerfield, her mother's fingers pressing into her shoulder, and knows that it was the last sound he ever made.

. . .

There are fewer and fewer people in the village in the weeks following the Harvest Festival. Kenniontie is back, but Atironta and the grown men are gone most of the time, hunting in the mountains, though some men stay on because of Queen Anne's war. Now there are peace negotiations going on. Atironta comes and goes, bringing fresh meat with him when he arrives. They have stored up dried meat, cornmeal, and acorns that have to be soaked, boiled, and pounded before they can be eaten. Hard work for not very tasty food, thinks A'onote. There is corn stored for seed as well, but Kenniontie tells her not to pop it over the fire except at the Midwinter Festival. They must save enough for planting in the spring. Gaianniana comes over sometimes, but other days she has only Ohnwatsihon to play with.

Today, A'onote doesn't mind so much. She has been learning new stories over the winter, and she likes to tell them in her own way, which she can do with Ohnwatsihon. When he tires of the games she invents for him, Ohnwatsihon is a good listener. They have been playing a game with their cornhusk dolls on a bearskin that they have rumpled up to make mountains and caves, but Tsihon has just squashed one of the mountains with her paws, and Onwatsihon is losing interest.

"I'll tell you the story about the Dancing Children," says A'onote. "Once, very long ago, long, long before the Great Peace of the Haudenosaunee, soon after Sky Woman fell to earth, and all the people began to appear, there were eight children who traveled a long way with their people, through the snowy mountains and along a great frozen river, until they came to a place that the women said was beautiful and good for planting everything they needed. But sometimes the children wanted to go off on their own and play. They found a special place they liked to go, where the moss was soft under their feet and beautiful tall cedar trees with red trunks surrounded them. Why did they like to go there, Ohnwatsihon? Do you know?"

"They had a happy dance," he answers.

"Yes, they had a very happy dance all their own. Shall we do it?"

And they get up and dance for a few minutes before she goes on with the story.

"Now, they liked to do this dance every day," she continues. "But sometimes they got hungry for more than the pemmican and maple sugar candy they brought with them, and one day a little boy—he looked just like you, Ohnwatsihon—suggested that they beg their parents to give them food to have a feast with their dancing. What happens next?"

"The feathered man says, 'No!'" shouts Ohnwatsihon.

"*Ok'e*! The strange, feathered man tells them they have to stop dancing the happy dance or bad things will happen. But they don't believe him, so they go to their parents to ask for food. And those parents say, 'No!' to the feast, just like the feathered man said to the dancing. They say the children can feast just as well at home."

"And they go!"

"Yes. They go without a feast, because they love to dance the happy dance. And they have so much fun that they find they can't stop dancing. The parents come and try to bring them home, but they just keep dancing."

"And they bring the feast."

"So the parents bring a whole feast, but the children don't want it anymore. They just keep dancing until finally they dance right up into the sky, where we can look at them in the winter. The parents keep coming back and raising offerings to the sky, but the children are happy up there, and only one little boy decides to come down. When you see a falling star in the winter, it is that little boy. It's dark now. Shall we see if they are out dancing?"

. . .

In the morning, Kenniontie fries corncakes before she and Asientie go off to a meeting of the Women's Council. A'onote finally asks the question that has been nagging at her for weeks. They are settled into the winter routine, sewing clothes, making wampum with the shells and beads they'd traded for throughout the year, telling stories by the fire, and going to the new chapel that the men have built in the village for the meeting she has learned to call the Mass.

"Why did Onnontio's wife want to see me?" she asks.

"She is interested in your welfare, A'onote. Many people are interested in your well-being."

"Why did you not let me meet her then?" A'onote looks closely at Kenniontie.

"If I and our chiefs say that you are well, there is no reason for Onnontio or his wife to be worried. We should be taken at our word."

"Did my father send her?"

"The Reverend Williams is far to the north with the priests in Quebec. He too has been assured you are well. Onnontio sees you as part of this war of Queen Anne's. He would like to use you to get some of his own people back from the English prisons. But you are one of us now. And your place with us is an honored one. You will see. We do not see you as one who can be traded."

A'onote holds out a basket for the fried cake Kenniontie offers her. Still, she thinks, her father *might* have sent Onnontio's wife. She would like to think so.

"Would you like to come and listen at the Women's Council for a little while today?" asks Kenniontie. This is an extraordinary offer to a nine-year-old. Gaianniana, who is ten, has only visited once. A'onote knows many girls aren't even allowed to visit before they have lived fifteen winters and danced with the women.

"Yes, I would," she answers eagerly.

"I can only let you stay for the early discussion, but I think it's a good idea to let you see a little of what goes on with us when we have earned our names and danced with the women. You will leave when the all the younger women go. It would not do to have you there when we discuss the chiefs. Get yourself ready now."

．　．　．

There are three fires and many women in the Council house. Asientie and Kenniontie settle themselves with A'onote at the large center fire. She knows that the senior women of the council have the power not only to appoint chiefs and declare war, but they can remove a chief from his seat if he has not acted according to the laws set down at the time of the Great Peace. A'onote is surprised to see Gentiyo at one of the smaller fires but remembers that she is older than Gaianniana.

A'onote is proud when Asientie is the first woman to speak, calling the meeting to order and introducing her as her granddaughter. Asienite asks her to stand.

"I am honored to visit the Women's Council," A'onote tells the assembly of women. She does feel honored and a little nervous too. Gaianniana will be impressed, she thinks.

Asientie, as the elder, continues speaking, recounting some of the recent events in Kahnawake—births, deaths, and marriages, reports from some of the men in the hunting camps. "There is more talk between the French and the English, which makes travel safer," she says. "But the war between them goes on in Europe, since both the Sun King, Louis XIV, and Queen Anne want to control the Spanish throne. Our lands are still part of their battleground, since they would like to control these too. There could be more surprise attacks in the spring, like the one on Port Royal. We must try not to let the European wars tear apart our own Great Peace," she continues. "Our Canienga cousins to the south see their interests as allied with their English neighbors, just as we see ours as with the French. It is a fine line we must walk to keep the peace among ourselves. We must discuss this and counsel our chiefs according to our discussion, if we are to preserve ourselves and the Haudenosaunee Peace."

A few more women speak, and then there is a general movement in the room, and Kenniontie bends down to her and tells her it is time to go. There is a short farewell speech and thanks given to all who have come, before many of the women and older girls file out.

As they come out into the cold, A'onote catches up to Gentiyo, whose seat was nearer the entrance to the council house. They are both wrapped in patterned blankets and their breath makes clouds as they speak. "You must have been surprised to see me, Gentiyo," she says. "I was surprised to see you. Kenniontie says it is a rare treat to come to the Council before dancing with the women. Have you come here before?"

"Twice," answers Gentiyo. "The first time there was a ceremony to welcome me. But I will not be able to come regularly until I have danced with the women at the Green Corn Festival next year. My brother Joseph was here a few days ago. He only stayed overnight. He goes everywhere now, trading, trading, trading!" She laughs. "His Huron master set him free, and he seems to be very good at it."

"If he's such a trader, maybe he'll want to trade for you," A'onote says, thinking again of Onnontio's wife.

"And then what would I do? All he does is travel, and I don't want to go back to Deerfield. I will have a field of my own to tend here, and I am happier here than I ever was before." This is something A'onote has not thought about. Is she also happier? Some days she is happy, but other days, even with her friends, she feels alone.

CHAPTER 13

The lull in the fighting during negotiations between Canada and the English colonies holds through the spring and into the summer. Now the Green Corn Festival is coming again, A'onote's third at Kahnawake. Joseph Kellogg has already come and gone several times, and Gaianniana's cousin Arosen is back at Kahnawake. Heading into her tenth winter, A'onote has been to the fields more often, both with Kenniontie and with Gentiyo and Gaianniana. She has seen how the women work together. The small mounds of earth they prepare for the corn, beans, and squash seeds remain from the year before. The farmwork is not as heavy as it seemed in Deerfield, since they don't have to plow the land. Wildflowers and meadow weeds, even strawberries and low-bush blueberries, grow between the mounds, and butterflies and bees hover over milkweed, sunflower, and thistle.

Now the beans twine themselves around the young cornstalks, and the squash vines blossom and tumble from the tops of the mounds. A'onote and Kenniontie are working quietly together, gathering beans and the early squash and corn. This is the easiest part of the season, since all but some late planting is done, and the corn has barely ripened. At this time of year, the plants seem to get along on their own, and it is almost like picking wild fruits. A'onote hears bits of talk and laughter from a nearby field, and occasionally someone stops to ask them how their crops are doing, but Kenniontie seems occupied by her own thoughts. Finally, she stands straight and rubs her neck, looking thoughtfully at A'onote.

"You know, A'onote. There is a man in Montreal who would like to see you. A John Sheldon from Guerrefille. Do you remember him?"

"No." She hesitates, wondering about her father. "Does the Reverend Williams send him?"

"It is Governor Dudley of Massachusetts who sends him."

She has heard the name Dudley in relation to the war. So it is not her father. "Do you want me to see him?" asks A'onote, thinking it is unlikely.

"It is not so much that I want you to see him, but he wants to see you, and I will allow it, if you agree." Kenniontie is quiet for a moment. "He wants to ask you if you will let him take you to Massachusetts with him."

"And you will let him take me away?" A'onote suddenly feels angry.

"We will never let anyone take you away from us, A'onote." Kenniontie puts both her hands on A'onote's shoulders. "Your roots are now as deep as those of the Great Peace. I do not believe you would leave us now. I trust you and believe you will choose wisely."

"I don't want to see him."

"It is better if you do," says Kenniontie quietly, and returns to her picking.

A'onote wants to ask who will come with her if she goes to see this man, and where she will meet him, but the subject seems closed for now. She is confused and frightened, almost dizzy, as if the soft, giving earth she stands on is dropping away. The sweet scent of squash blossoms and clover overwhelms her.

"I don't want to pick anymore," she tells Kenniontie.

"You can go back to the longhouse or go find Gaianniana or Gentiyo," says Kenniontie. "Don't worry about this man. He has no power here."

. . .

The next day, after lessons in the mission house, Achiendase walks along with her. "Do you say your beads regularly?"

A'onote nods. It is true that she says the beads, though not exactly regularly. But sometimes the whole world seems strange to her, and she finds the prayers comforting.

"You know that Kenniontie and Atironta promised Onnontio that they will let you speak to this man who is coming to see you and that they will let you go with him if you ask them to. They would not do this, if they didn't know your heart and trust in you, A'onote. You will meet him here tomorrow. Kenniontie and I will both be with you. He cannot take you away with him, unless you ask him to." A'onote looks up at him, expecting to hear more. "I must return to the mission now. Just remember, your life will be very different if you go, A'onote. And they will not like you to pray to Our Mother in Heaven."

Far ahead on the path, just entering the woods between the mission and Kahnawake, she sees Gentiyo, Gaianniana, Arosen, and few others. She doesn't pause to think, but runs as fast as she can to catch up to them. No one asks her what the priest said, and she has no wish to tell them. It would make her feel like an outsider.

. . .

When she goes to the mission house the next day, there is nothing familiar about John Sheldon, who is tall and red-faced from the sun. She does not like the smell that clings about his clothes. He seems to have nothing to do with her or her father, and it surprises her that she only understands some of his words. Achiendase has to tell her some of it in the Canienga language. She does not care what he says and does not say a word, only shakes her head and turns to leave when he asks if she will go with him.

She is relieved as she and Kenniontie head back to work in the fields and glad to see Gaianniana and Gentiyo helping out there too. The corn, beans, and squash all come in together. Joining the other girls, it suddenly strikes her that they themselves are like the three sisters.

. . .

By the time the Harvest Moon has come and gone, all negotiations between the English and the French have been broken off. A'onote feels a moment of relief—no more visitors from Deerfield—and then a twinge of regret.

Falling into step with Arosen near her house one day, A'onote is curious at how he manages to travel between the territories so easily.

"Gaianniana says you are going back to spend some time with your family down at Canajoharie Castle," she begins. "Isn't it dangerous for you now that the French and English are back at war?"

"We have to be able to move among our own people," he answers. "This war won't be settled until the war in Europe ends. And who knows whether it will be over then. The English want Canada for themselves. I don't think they'll stop until they get it."

"You think this land will belong to England someday?"

"I think it will," answers Arosen.

A'onote is lost in thought for a moment, unsure what this might mean for her. She looks up at Arosen and notices again the sharp, narrow scar on his handsome cheek. "You haven't said if it's dangerous for you to go south," she repeats.

"Alone, I am no threat, and the English can't be sure if I am someone they could get payment for," he replies. "Anyway, the prisoner exchanges have stopped. I'm probably safer than ever."

"You come here so often. Do you like Kahnawake or the English country better?" They have stopped at the rock in front of the longhouse.

"The English colonies seem to belong more and more to the English, while there seems more room for our people up here. I like to keep a foot in both worlds," Arosen says. "I'll be back, A'onote. Stay well."

CHAPTER 14

A'onote's fourth Green Corn Festival arrives. Her tenth winter has passed, and still so many to go before she can dance with the women. Yesterday, Achiendase baptized Gentiyo in a ceremony in the chapel. She has fifteen winters now and will be called Marie Gentiyo. Today A'onote and Gaianniana will watch her dance with the women for the first time. It is early, and a red sun tops the horizon, making a glittering path that stretches across the wide bend in the rapids. Its rays reach through the trunks of the cedars to warm the girls, who have made their bed beneath the trees in preparation for the beginning of the festival.

A'onote sits up and strokes Tsihon, who opens a lazy eye and promptly closes it again. A'onote blows lightly on her friend's forehead, but Gaianniana just turns her head away. Then she prods her with a toe, but gets no response at all. Finally, A'onote roots around in the satchel beside her and finds a feather to tickle her with.

"Wake up, silly one, I have to comb your hair! Gaia! Gaia! Wake up!"

Gaianniana sits up looking grumpy and irritated for a moment, then grabs the feather away and tries to tickle her back. They are still laughing as they open the satchels they packed yesterday with clothes, beads, and ribbons to wear for the ceremony.

Atironta smiles as he approaches and and sits to chat with them for a few minutes. He has been away from Kahnawake often since the Very Cold Moon at midwinter, first hunting, then fishing and trading near Canajoharie Castle. Now he and the rest of the grown men seem to be resting up for the next winter, making music, carving bowls and cradle boards, and spending time with A'onote and her friends. It seems a long time since her first Green Corn Festival, but A'onote is still surprised by how Atironta takes his time, resting and playing during the summer. There is a part of her that always expects a scolding for being idle.

"Be careful," jokes Atironta, "If you make your braids too beautiful, the little people of the darkness, the *odowah*, will think you have strawberries in your hair and try to steal them!" And he gives one of Gaia's half-finished braids a tweak.

"If they do, the good *jogoah* will steal them back for us," laughs Gaianniana. A'onote is puzzled, but when Gaianniana begins to remind her of the stories of the little people from above and below the earth Atironta interrupts her.

"Save up some stories for the winter storytelling," he tells her. "Now finish up and see if the women need your help this morning. I'll look for you in the children's dance."

When they have finished dressing, the girls wrap their belongings in the skins they slept on, tuck them into the crook of a tree, and leave their encampment to head for the village center. As they enter the leafy avenue where the plums begin to ripen, they see Arosen, tall and dark, talking with Marie Gentiyo's brother Joseph. At fourteen, Joseph seems grown. He is always full of tales about his travels as a trader among the many tribes of Indians, and the English, French, and Dutch. Deep in conversation with Arosen he does not immediately notice A'onote and Gaianniana.

"I plan to travel west after the Green Corn Festival. The voyageur Lejeune arrived here last night and plans to keep us company. There is no shortage of furs in the West. And I want to see the western country." There is a little swagger in Joseph's voice, but he speaks with authority. Arosen is quieter.

Looking thoughtfully at A'onote, Joseph grins. "You look ready for the dancing!" He says in the Canienga tongue. It is rude to speak English among people who do not. "We will look for you in the children's dance, when we have finished our gaming."

A'onote watches him admiringly as he walks away with Arosen. She wonders whether Stephen's life might be like his, and anything seems possible.

Later in the afternoon, A'onote and Gaianniana watch excitedly as Gentiyo joins the women in their dance circling the fire with a proud, stately gait. She wears the multicolored shift that she worked on all winter, striped with shiny ribbons that match the beads in her hair. She looks so beautiful that A'onote forgets for the moment about the children's dance. Four years seems a long time to wait, but the girls can't join the dance until they have fifteen winters behind them. A'onote, who has nearly eleven winters, looks over at Gaianiana, who is less than a year older and wonders whether she looks as grown up as Gaia does and whether Joseph and Arosen will really come to the children's dance.

· · ·

"You are a pretty dancer, Marie Gentiyo," A'onote calls out a week later as they head for the mission. Gaianniana does not seem to go as often as she used to, and no one else from A'onote's family is going today, so she is on her own. "You looked beautiful dancing with the women."

"I was very happy," says Gentiyo.

"Joseph said he would come to watch us in the children's dance, but he never did."

"*Ai*! Joseph. He wanders. Not only his feet but his mind. I'm sure he meant to go, A'onote, but he got involved with something else and forgot. He has always been like this, very good at whatever he is working on, but not so good at remembering what he should move on to. I think that's why this traveling and trading suits him."

"I didn't ask him to come." A'onote shrugs. "He looked right at me and said he would."

"You like my brother! I do too, but he makes very little time for anyone. That will change in time. Who knows? Maybe by the time you are old enough to have a suitor, Joseph will not be wandering. But you might like someone else better by then."

A'onote blushes. "Is there someone you like?" she asks.

"I'm as bad as Joseph. From one thing to another. Your young uncle, Tsiatekenha, likes me and I like him, but sometimes I think I like Atironta's friend Rowahokon. Arosen is very handsome, but he is only fifteen, no older than I am. Rowahokon is old enough to have made a name for himself. We shall see. I have plenty of time before I think about settling on one and marrying."

"Do you think you will marry here, now that you have danced with the women?" The thought is entirely new and surprising. She has imagined dancing with the women and joining the Women's Society, even becoming a healer in the Otter Society like Kenniontie and Asientie. It has never occurred to her that she, or even Gentiyo, would marry here. She hasn't thought about marriage at all.

"If I marry, it will be here, but I don't think I'll marry before the next Green Corn Festival. Maybe not even then. I'm happy as I am." A'onote wonders if Atironta and the council of chiefs would allow Gentiyo to marry someone as young as Arosen. Fifteen or not, they remain her playmates.

"And would you be married in the chapel by Achiendase?" asks A'onote as they approach the tall building.

"Yes. I am a Catholic now."

"Do you think Gaia will marry in the chapel someday too?"

"That I can't say. She may follow Asientie's way and be married in the longhouse. And you, what do you think you'll do?"

"I don't know." It is a puzzle to her that she likes Achiendase and some of the ways of his church, in spite of all her father told her when she saw him.

The next day Joseph is gone, and A'onote is disappointed. Once again, he has left without telling anyone his plans. Without ceremony, she thinks.

CHAPTER 15

As the harvest season comes on, talk of the war intensifies. Prisoner exchanges have ended, and Onnontio, the French governor, has asked the Kahnawake people to participate in attacks against the English along the border. Asientie, Kenniontie, and Sientiesie debate the question in the Women's Council and bring the discussion home with them. A'onote knows there is reluctance among the women to return to full-blown war, but other tribes are cooperating in the attacks. The question is especially disturbing to her. Since the war has heated up again, Kenniontie and Atironta have worried that the English might send spies to steal her back, now that there is no question of trading for her. It is getting hard to imagine another life.

Kenniontie and Sientiesie are discussing a trip to Montreal to do some trading for fancy fabrics, ribbons, lace, and buttons they will want to use in their sewing and weaving during the winter. A'onote loves everything about going to Montreal—negotiating the wild rapids, the first sight of the stone walls and the statue of Our Lady of Bon Secours, all the people, and the goods.

"Let me come too!" she begs.

"Not this time," answers Kenniontie. "Things are different now. I worry about English spies in the city."

"Why is it that Gentiyo can go where she wants without worry?"

"No one comes looking for Gentiyo. They do not seem to think there is much money in getting her back. There is a powerful minister in Boston, named Mather. Do you know his name?"

A'onote shakes her head.

"He has reasons for wanting to redeem the daughter of another minister. According to Achiendase, it is part of their religion," Kenniontie says with a wave of her hand. "Misfortune, such as losing a daughter, might reflect badly on the minister himself. Bringing you back would make their church look powerful. Gentiyo is not the daughter of a minister. Bringing her back would not make as good a story to support their church."

"If I stay close to you, nothing can happen to me. Or Atironta could come with us."

"A'onote hasn't spent much time out of Kahnawake," Atironta tells Kenniontie. "I would like to take her with me on a small hunting and trading expedition. We'll go no farther than the tip of the long lake and make our camps carefully."

After a great deal of discussion and some intervention by Asientie, who does not want her to grow up fearful, A'onote is allowed to go, proud to be setting off with Atironta alone, so that he will rely on her as his helper in making and breaking their camps, and even in hunting, since Kenniontie has insisted that she not be alone for a minute.

. . .

One night, A'onote looks up at Atironta as she fashions a little spit over the fire to cook some grouse he has snared for dinner. "This is like being with you on the way to Kahnawake," she says. "I was little then, but I still remember you showing me how to make the fires and cook the meat you brought back. It made me feel safe somehow."

"I hoped it would," says Atironta. "I could see that you were very quick and curious and would like to learn. You have proven it ever since. You know, Kenniontie and Asientie would like to start teaching you about their medicine soon. They see that you have a gift, and each has her own medicine to teach you. They expect you will join the Otter Society as a healer someday after you earn your new name and dance. It takes years of work, but you are surely up to it. They are as proud of you as I am."

That night she falls asleep still glowing with happiness.

• • •

The next morning they uncover the canoe that has been stashed near the French fort and begin paddling. They head toward the English trading post that sits between the large lake Champlain and the narrow lake below it. The strip of land that divides the two lakes is the door between Canada and the English colonies. Sometimes the door is open wide, but now there is just a crack to slip through.

The journey has taken them six days. While there has been no snow, there is a suggestion of it in the air. They can see smoke curling from a number of small Abenaki villages that dot the shore on the far side of the lake. Those villages belong to the people that Stephen was last seen with, she thinks. It just might be possible that he will be at the trading post, that she might see him, just as

Gentiyo sees her brother Joseph. But she does not want to tell Atironta that she is looking for her brother.

"When we come to the fort, we must look for Joseph Kellogg. I promised Gentiyo I would tell him she is marrying Tsiatekenha at the Midwinter Festival."

"We will look, my little otter cub," replies Atironta, using one of his fond nicknames for her. "But if he's there, he will find us soon enough. The little people speak to that young man. He has ears all over the country and will have heard that his sister is marrying. No worrying. Whether we meet him here or not, he will be sure to be with us at midwinter. Now, we are close to English country. Don't wander off looking for Joseph. At the fort and all around it you must stay with me."

A'onote nods and thinks about how Atironta and Kenniontie worry when she travels with them. She has been told so many times that she is planted in their hearts. They are now planted in her heart too. Yet there is always the question: What if her father comes for her?

Looking down the lake, she can see traders setting up on the shore. As the canoe crests the waves, she digs into the whitecaps with barely a splash. Canoes and wide French bateaux dot the water with splotches of color from piles of clothes and blankets.

Despite the sunless day, the scene on the shore in front of the fort is almost as colorful as the landing at Montreal. Atironta scans the crowd cautiously as they disembark, and then greets Rowahokon, a younger man who is as tall and as powerfully built as he is. "Greetings, Wolf brother!" They clap hands on one another's shoulders. Then Rowahokon turns to her and does the same, calling her Sister Turtle, for the clan of her mothers.

"Your trade goods are where I told you." Rowahokon gestures

with his chin. "So many people. Good to trade quickly and be gone."

"We can meet in the lower meadow and travel back together tomorrow," suggests Atironta.

"There are pretty things here, A'onote. Choose wisely, and make your mother happy," Rowahokon says cheerfully, and opens a fist, disclosing a smooth soapstone whistle delicately shaped and gray as the sky. "For you, from brothers far to the south. Made long ago."

She thanks him gravely, like an adult. As she opens her palm, her shawl falls open revealing the fancy quill and beadwork on her tunic. Rowahokon looks at her, and she suddenly feels much older than her eleven years, as if she could dance with the women. She remembers Gentiyo, shrugging and saying she liked Rowahokon, but Gentiyo has chosen Tsiatekehna. They take leave of each other, Rowahokon heading into the crowd with a slight limp from the broken leg she knows he suffered as a captive among the Southern Canienga when the Great Peace was broken years before.

Returning with their pelts and wampum after leaving Rowahokon, A'onote and Atironta are both attracted to a stack of folded cloth in myriad colors piled on the beach around a Dutch trader's boat. Atironta unbundles some beaver pelts from the West that he had traded for in an earlier trip to Montreal and spreads them out for the man's inspection. A'onote looks through the pile of fabrics thinking of clothes for the Midwinter Festival. Kneeling, she lifts her gaze to find it caught up by the inquiring blue eyes of a small, stocky Dutchman who has wandered over as if he too were interested in their wares. Surprised at the intensity of his look, she turns quickly to Atironta, her words tumbling out awkwardly.

"My mother would like this cloth." She lifts a pale, heavy woolen.

"It is good quality and we could have enough for all of us." But suddenly her eye falls on a blue wool fabric trimmed in red, the color of a robin's egg and the color, too, of Kateri Tekakwitha's robe in a painting at the mission. "Oh, this is beautiful! I would take this above everything the man has brought to trade."

When Atironta nods, the Dutchman addresses him, gesturing toward A'onote.

"Is this an English child?"

A'onote is not sure what language he is speaking. She understands only the word "English" and looks questioningly at Atironta and back to the man, avoiding his eyes but noticing a small moon-shaped scar on his chin.

"This child is Canienga," replies Atironta in his own tongue, and turning back to the trader, he nods toward the blue stroud A'onote has chosen. "We would have that blue stroud for one of these skins."

"Surely the child is English. Will she understand me if I speak English to her?" repeats the Dutchman, his English sounding more foreign than the French A'onote hears in Montreal.

"*Jagoghte*," says Atironta with a small shrug of his shoulder. The phrase, meaning *maybe not*, is understood by most colonists to mean *no*.

"Will you allow me to question her?"

Atironta nods assent with an air of indifference.

"Do you know the name Eunice?" The pale man is both kind and businesslike, with a complacent air about him. Atironta dwarfs him, and A'onote herself could almost meet his eye at a level, if she wished to. She does not. She hears the name Eunice and knows it, but it does not seem like her own. She shivers as it sinks in that not a single word, not even the way he says her name, sounds familiar.

"The Reverend John Williams of Deerfield is your father?" She looks back at him now with narrowed eyes. Even this name sounds strange, although she knows it, and her heart lurches. She can feel its beat slow and quicken as he goes on speaking a language that she can't quite grasp.

"I represent Peter Schuyler of Albany." The man switches to the Canienga tongue. "If your master will allow it, I can return you to your father in Deerfield. It would rejoice your father and his new wife to see your exile ended." His words, though she understands them now, seem to come from very far away. "Your brothers and sister long for your return. Your sister has married, and you have two new half-brothers who have never seen you."

A'onote stares at the scar on his chin, her eyes straying back to the blue stroud. Tiny snowflakes begin dancing in the air, making little pinpricks of cold on her face. She looks at Atironta, and he looks back at her at her with concern.

"You understood him?"

She nods. Indeed, he spoke Canienga clearly. Yet she can hardly take in what he has said. Her father and his *wife*? Her whole Engish family in Guerrefille and her father married? "Do you want to go with this man?" Atironta asks. She takes several slow steps back, as if a bear with young had appeared in her path.

"I am at your service." The man looks strangely at her now, and he bows with measured politeness. "I carry both goods and messages, an ambassador of a kind. . . . Most traders know about you. Most will bring messages if you ask. At your service." He manages to catch her eye before turning away.

Atironta returns to his business and finishes his barter quickly, pinching his nostrils as they leave. "Pfft! They smell!" He says as soon as they are out of earshot. "What do they do to stink like that?"

A'onote shrugs. They are leaving with her blue stroud, striped red at the edges; a salmon and white calico; some fine lace trim; and some buttons. They have done well and still have wares to trade, so they move on in search of other goods. But the Dutch trader's words shadow her. The man (she tucks the name Schuyler away) said her father was in Guerrefille, that he took everyone but her home with him. And he has a wife. He would not have married. It's all a lie, she thinks. But she is deeply shaken. What if it is true?

CHAPTER 16

A'onote cannot not bring herself to ask Atironta about her English family, and she is not sure that he would know the truth. She returns to Kahnawake carrying a new weight. There has been snow since they left and, two nights after her return, the Northern Lights unfurl an astonishing display, stroking the sky with bands of shimmering green diffusing into pink as they reach up toward the stars. Most of the village has turned out to watch. The glaze on the snow glows, crisscrossed with stuttering shadows. Wrapped in buffalo robes and blankets, A'onote, Ohnwatshihon, Gaianniana, and Gentiyo huddle together, trying to guess one another's dreams, a midwinter custom.

Winter nights bring A'onote's favorite constellation, the children who danced their way into the sky, but tonight the sky seems more alien than beautiful to her. It makes her feel as if the world she knows is slipping away. Marie Gentiyo and Tsiatekenha celebrated their marriage in the chapel yesterday, even though Gentiyo had told A'onote that she would not marry before the next Green

Corn Festival. Watching her dance far into the night with her new husband A'onote felt betrayed by the happiness around her.

Joseph Kellogg did not return for his sister's wedding. The trap lines of rumor that run along the trade routes from the West have it that he has traveled into a far country with the voyageur Lejeune. Ohnwatsihon talks about Joseph constantly, enamored of his imagined exploits. A'onote, however, is disturbed by Joseph's absence and thinks he must not approve of Gentiyo's marriage. "I wonder whether you will dance with the women," he had said to A'onote with a frown after watching Gentiyo dance last summer. Now, she wonders if he had heard something about her father or this man, Schuyler, looking for her.

All afternoon, through the first of the winter games, she had looked for Joseph, though no one else expected him. When the last game of snow snakes ended, and the boys began to put away their javelins, while gamblers collected or paid their debts, A'onote stood in the graying snow and gave up.

Now the moon rises, a mother of pearl disk on the eastern horizon, Sky Woman's pendant, reflecting the strange lights. The gaudy sky has set the wolves crooning. Tsihon growls and raises her head, whining and yipping in response to her wild cousins. A'onote opens her robe and enfolds the dog to share her warmth.

"You want to sing with the wolves," she says. "Stay here by me."

"Let me guess your dream," says Gentiyo, her face changing in the light. "I can see that you have had one."

"Give us a hint so we can discover it for you," adds Gaianniana. "I know that Gentiyo is right. You have dreamed something."

A'onote is startled. She has in fact had a disturbing dream the night before.

"Tsihon knows my dream," says A'onote with a shiver, and snuggles up to her dog.

"It is a dream about the Wolf Clan," hazards Ohnwatsihon excitedly. He is now in his seventh winter, about the same age A'onote was when she first came to Kahnawake. "Maybe you will marry a member of the Wolf Clan. Maybe Joseph Kellogg."

"You're silly," says Gaianniana scornfully. "Joseph is not of the Wolf Clan, and A'onote does not even dance in the women's dance. She would not be dreaming that." Gaianniana tosses her hair behind her shoulders and resettles her fur hat. "*You* might dream that because you would like to see Joseph in your longhouse, but A'onote would not be dreaming it. Joseph is far away. Will he come back? He might even have returned to the English by now."

A'onote is startled. "Why would you say that? He may be here tomorrow. Rowahokon has not come back from hunting either. Do you think *he* is staying among the English?" Even in the cold her face is flaming.

Gentiyo looks at her curiously. "My brother may not return," she says quietly, and returns to the dream guessing. "The white dog that will be sacrificed to end the midwinter ceremony? Is that in it?"

"The dog is not in it." A'onote shrugs beneath her blanket. "Or maybe it is. I don't remember." She is surprised to hear Gentiyo say that Joseph might not come back. It pains her in a way that keeps her from asking why. The green arcs in the north go on flickering above the horizon. She thinks she could pluck the pendant moon from the sky, it seems so sharp and separate.

"Tsihon whines at the wolves. Maybe there is a wolf in it. A dying wolf?" suggests Gaianniana. Surprised, A'onote says nothing.

Gentiyo lifts her head in response. "I saw you once, A'onote. It was a very long time ago. In Guerrefille. I was walking along the road with my mother and we saw you at the meetinghouse door. You were so little, and you were by yourself. You were looking up at a wolf's head hung on the hook above you. Someone had nailed its head to the door to collect the bounty. It was an awful thing to look at, scary."

A'onote straightens up in surprise, letting her blankets fall away for a moment. "I remember the wolves' heads, but I don't remember being there by myself."

She thinks about the bloody, drooling heads nailed to the once-familiar door, smells the blood, and sees the crawling yellow eye, the crows gathering on the bare branches of a winter tree.

Gaianniana looks at her closely, "They must be ugly people who would nail wolves' heads to a door, giving them no respect in death. Wolves should be killed only in the worst of times. When they are too many and not enough food. I know the meaning of this dream," she continues, her voice gathering a shrill edge. "It only means that the English spirit has died in you and that the white dog sacrifice will banish it forever." She takes a breath. "It means," she says in more measured tones, "that your English family has long since returned to their own country, where they cut the heads off of wolves and take scalps for bounty. They will not come back here. We must get tobacco for you to burn at the white dog offering. That is all. The dream will go away."

"That was not well spoken." Gentiyo looks at Gaianniana steadily. "Why would you say that to us?"

A'onote is stunned into silence by Gaianniana's words. She has suspected it might be true that her English family has returned to the colonies. She has often thought herself abandoned, but never heard it said until Schuyler's man told her that her father was in Guerrefille. Again, she sees her father as he was in Montreal, his strange, ill-fitting suit, and the way he seemed to shrink from her there on the busy street. He abandoned her mother to a cruel death. She had not been able to make him wait. Of course he would return to the colonies without coming to her. Of course he would take her siblings and begin a whole new family. It was written long before. The sky's display seems wearying. She shrugs Gentiyo's hand away. She wants to return to the longhouse and be swallowed in sleep. The universe, so strangely lit, is vast and lonely.

A'onote thinks of her mother. She sees her blue cloak, red hair. If she could just see her mother's eyes she would be happy. Once she asked Marie Gentiyo what she remembered of her mother from their days in Guerrefille. "Hair like a fox," Marie said, after thinking for a moment. "Your mother sat with mine for a very long time when my mother's last baby was born. I thought my mother would die. But your mother told me not to worry, that it was a difficult birth, but my mother was fine and I had a new brother. I didn't care about the brother then. She had a pretty voice, your mother." A'onote is jealous of Marie Gentiyo's memory. She cannot hear her mother's voice.

The longhouse is cold and empty when she and Ohnwatsihon get there. Even Asientie is still at the dream guessing. She leads the sleepy boy over to the closet he shares with Sientiesie and pulls the blankets up around him. Then, lonely herself, she crawls in next to him and tells him a story of the good *jogoah*, the little people who help. She makes it a funny story about their battles with the mischievous *odowah* and has them bring strawberries to Ohnwatsihon at midwinter.

The boy falls asleep, but A'onote does not. She tries to push her pain away from her, but behind every pain is another. She still doesn't know if the Reverend really has a new wife. But he returned to Guerrefille with the others. He hadn't even come back to see her before he left. He hadn't ever come back for her at all.

. . .

When she gets up in the morning, A'onote feels a weight dropping out of her center. She is surprised to find herself still in Sientiesie's sleeping closet, Ohnwatsihon sleeping beside her, and Sientiesie on his other side. She eases herself out of the bed, tucking the blankets around him. She pulls on her moccasins and wraps her blue blanket around her, throwing the end over her shoulder. It is earlier than she thought. She throws a few sticks on the fire to keep it going and heads outside. Clouds have moved in with the dawn. It is a little warmer and feels like snow. It is hard to believe she is looking at the same sky as the night before. She feels curiously light as she heads for a thicket, shaky and quivery as she crouches behind a bush to relieve herself. As she rises she notices red spots on the snow. Berries brushed from a nearby bush, she thinks. Then, with a panicky flutter in her chest, she looks down at the tops of her legs. There is a pale wash where her thighs meet. Something is wrong, she thinks. Maybe I'm sick. But then she knows what it is. She takes a handful of snow to cleanse herself. Despite the fact that Gaianniana has already been bleeding each moon for some time now, she had not expected it to come to her so soon. She is only eleven.

A'onote still has a small seat in another world, and this passage seems to make it smaller still. She feels light-headed and finds that she is crying. She doesn't want to tell anyone; she already feels so alone. It is going to snow and she doesn't want to go off by herself to fast for days, as is the ritual. What if the snow comes hard, and she is hungry and alone and covered over? She tries to remember if her mother and sister in Guerrefille retreated from the house for days every month. It doesn't seem so; she and Gentiyo have never spoken of that. Would Ohnwatsihon be hurt, being so close to her when it began? She knows that she has a special power now, as Kenniontie and Sientiesie do each moon, when they sleep away from the longhouse for a few days. If she tries to hide it, she can bring terrible misfortune on her family. She is not sure that she can even enter the house again today. The proper thing is to be alone and use the time for reflection.

A'onote pulls her blanket tighter around her as she steps back onto the path to the house. She looks again at the sky and the bare groves of plum trees. She is afraid, but at the same time she feels her mind and body quit of a weight that has been building in her. When she reaches home, she sits on the rock a little way from the longhouse and waits. She wonders how far away they will build her wigwam. Again, she thinks of the women of Guerrefille. What did her mother do?

It is not long before Asientie comes out of the house and sees her sitting forlornly on the rock. She bursts into tears as she tells her.

"It is wonderful!" the old woman cries. "We will build you a hut not too far off from the house," she continues reassuringly, as she looks at the sky. "You will have no reason to fear the snow."

She goes in to tell Kenniontie, who comes hurrying out of the house. "So your *onnigaensa* has arrived. You are a woman. It is good. You will see."

A'onote is heartened by the women's enthusiasm. They return with a bearskin robe for her to sit on while they collect poles for the hut from the side of the house where they keep wood for the fire and outdoor tools. They head into the orchard and spread the bearskin on the snow again for her to sit on.

As if by magic, Gaianniana appears in the orchard a few minutes later. Ordinarily this is something they would share, but A'onote is still angry about what Gaianniana said the night before. She knows it is the truth, but she turns away.

"I see that something new has happened. This is a great thing! Sientiesie told me you were here," says Gaianniana, sitting down anyway. "I brought you something. I am sorry I hurt you last night." She holds out a lovely strip of beadwork as a peace offering, and continues more quietly, "I said that about the English because I have been afraid you will go away. I was more afraid than ever when I heard that your father and your brothers had gone, and I was afraid that you would go too." Gaianniana gets up to help the women, while A'onote takes in what she has just understood— that Gaia knew that her English family had returned to Guerre- fille without coming for her. It is a blow to think how little her father must love her and that everyone here must know it. Even Stephen, who always seemed somehow just out of sight, seems lost to her now.

"Don't be afraid," says Gaianniana when the hut is finished. They have built a small, sturdy wigwam covered with bark and skins, strong but easy to take apart when she is ready to leave it. "No harm will come to you. With the snow on the ground you won't have to be off by the river. The time will pass quickly. You will be surprised when it is over."

Kenniontie brings her a supply of dried moss saved from the summer and builds a fire inside, admonishing her to keep it going. She looks tenderly at A'onote and places her hand on her head.

"You will be sheltered here from the snow. It won't pile up too high, and the wind will not be strong. I know you are frightened. It is a surprise when it comes, but you will find that you are strong and you are wise. You will know, more than you do now, who you are." She looks at A'onote as if she would like to linger.

Gaianniana and Asientie each give her a hug, and Gaianniana's mother, who has joined them now, gives her a small talisman. Asientie runs a hand along her face before departing, the dry hand seeming to leave a silky streak along A'onote's cheek.

Then A'onote is alone in her shelter. On the side facing the orchard, a blanket is pushed aside so she can see out during the day when it is not too cold. The bearskin is now spread inside. The fire is dry and not too smoky. She sits looking out. Pine saplings poke their way through the snow in places. Beyond that the winter orchard falls away from her. She is strangely glad that everyone is gone. Bright jays chatter in the trees.

Gaianniana and her mother brought her beads and porcupine quills and other materials to work with, but anything she makes will have to go into her medicine bag in Asientie's carved chest where she keeps the silver cup her mother gave her, for it will be considered sacred work. The snow has not yet begun to fall, but the world is quiet and waiting, each sound clear and distinct. There will be bonfires tonight, bigger than her little wigwam, as the Midwinter Festival goes on. There will be feasting and storytelling, and no one will wander out to her orchard. She selects some beads to add to a quillwork design she is planning. She looks down at her quillwork. *The same*, a voice inside her says. *I am the same*. She has always liked colors and designs, always enjoyed her needlework.

She sees herself standing behind a chair and Esther standing too. The men are seated—her father, Samuel, and someone else, her oldest brother perhaps. There is food on the trestle and the grownups are passing it around and eating, while she and her siblings stand behind the chairs and wait to be served. Could that be right?

But she knows it is. Were Parthena and Frank standing there too? She can't remember. We were a little like the dogs the way we got our food, she thinks. We had no seat, she thinks, and smiles to her herself; the literal truth meets so neatly the Canienga phrase for having one's place and honor. She had always thought it was something about herself that made her father dismiss her. Perhaps her sister wasn't important either, or even her brothers while they were small. The most important thing about food in the world she inhabits is that it is shared equally with all present, even buried in snow for strangers to find when traveling. She remembers the scornful talk she has heard about the English. They want to treat with people they will not share a table with.

The heavy cloud cover makes it hard for A'onote to tell how much time has passed. She wishes she had eaten more yesterday. She goes to gather some kindling, walking toward a frozen stream at the far side of the orchard. A sleek marten with a small animal in its mouth darts away over the ice. Tsihon takes off after it and overtakes it. The marten escapes, but not with its prey, which Tsihon makes short work of. Pleased that the dog has had some food, she heads back toward her wigwam, thinking again of her mother.

Gentiyo said once that the women didn't have much in Guerrefille. They didn't own their houses or have councils or come together to choose leaders. They did their husbands' bidding, Gentiyo said. She was explaining why she would not want to leave with her brother. It didn't mean much to A'onote at the time, but she sees now that at Kahnawake she is Kenniontie's daughter, Asientie's granddaughter, a favored child of the tribe from whom much is expected.

As she turns away from the stream, the image of her mother flares with unusual vividness, as clear as the painting in the mission. Her bonnet, her red hair. For a moment she hears her mother's voice. Large, wet snowflakes begin to float around her as she approaches the wigwam. She pulls a blanket around her as she settles inside. There is no wind, and snow is falling thickly. She doesn't loosen the blanket to cover the entrance, doesn't want to shut out the dwindling light or feel shut in.

Feeding her small fire so that it leaps to life, A'onote thinks of her father's voice in the meetinghouse. Certainly there was no Heavenly Mother in her father's religion. Nothing associated with God was female. God had no mother in his stories. A'onote burrows into her blankets and thinks about Ataensic, the Canienga mother of all, whose light is reflected in all that glows. When she prays, it is usually to the Virgin Mother, Marie, but the two seem very much alike to her. Two faces of the same deity.

Tsihon nudges her hand for attention. The snow is so heavy now that it seems she can hear it falling from the trees. She puts a thick hickory knot on the fire and lets sleep steal over her. What comes is a light and hungry sleep. Her mother seems especially close. She can almost see her eyes. At one point she thinks there is something in the open doorway. She doesn't know whether she is asleep or awake. When she looks again, an otter stands upright in the doorway, singing a song that she can barely remember in the morning.

A'onote wakes up to a dull sun rising and a fresh blanket of snow drifting in the door, where she had not closed the flap the night before. Tsihon whines, and they step out carefully into an orchard blossoming with soft snow petals. She sweeps the feathery snow aside as she walks, trying to recapture the song that the otter person sang to her. All she can remember is *deyakodarakeh asatakon*, two clans in the dark, sung in a low, sweet voice.

By the third day it has turned colder again, and the

snowy orchard sparkles in the sun. A'onote is aware that she has been rehearsing the story of her life for days, as if she were composing it to tell to someone. She reaches the frozen stream, boundary of the world she inhabits for these few days. She turns back with a whistle to Tsihon. It seems that the world is sparkling with power today and that some of it belongs to her.

On her final night she dreams of the otter again, but this time its song is a happier one. "*Deskenonweronne*," sings the otter, standing upright in her doorway again, "I come again to greet and thank." But this time there are other otters standing behind her, singing. And in the dream this seems perfectly natural, because, unlike the marten, who hunts alone, otters are usually seen in families. The otter is inviting me, she thinks. I *will* become a healer like Asientie in the Otter Society.

PART IV

MARGUERITE
OCTOBER 1710–OCTOBER 1713

CHAPTER 17

Two more harvest moons have come and gone since peace talks ended. Queen Anne's War continues. A'onote can now count six harvests since she came to Kahnawake, three since she learned that her father and brothers had long since joined her older sister in Guerrefille, and that her father married soon after he returned. She is entering her fourteenth winter. As far as she knows, no one has come looking for her since she met the Dutch trader at the fort with Atironta. Now the door between the French and the English seems truly closed, though the Canienga people still seem to pass through it.

Since the taking of Port Royal on the coast by the English a month ago, Arosen, Gaianniana's handsome cousin with the scar on his cheek, comes often to talk with Atironta and Asientie. A'onote, who once considered him a friend, watches him warily as he and Atironta enter the longhouse and stand in the doorway talking. He is older now, already nineteen, and he adds to the restlessness that is welling up at Kahnawake. Uneasy questions ride the breezes, rustle among the falling leaves, and hint at coming changes.

"*Kayanerenh*," he greets A'onote, warmly as ever, but to her it seems a strange greeting, since it is a peaceful salute, and all the talk is of war.

"This victory and the queen's aid have given the English courage," Arosen tells Atironta. "There are English troops just below the door in the country, and some warriors from the Five Nations are joining them. Most of the Haudenosaunee League and all the rest of the Canienga people support the English. If the people of Kahwanake continue in their alliance with the French, it will be hard to maintain the Great Peace among us."

"We live among the French," answers Atironta, "and many of us share the French religion. We have agreements with them, just as others do with the English. The covenant chain we agreed on in the Great Peace allows us to forge our own alliances. But I admit we are of two minds. We are questioning all alliances."

"There are many questions," Atironta continues. "What is the Sun King in France doing for his children at Kahnawake, as he calls us? This long war takes a toll and divides us when we need strength."

A'onote melts into the shadows as they sit down at the hearth. Arosen and his conversation upset her. Why does he talk like a war chief? She slips away without a word and heads toward Gaianniana's house. Outside the pungent smell of sumac smoke permeates the autumn evening. Beyond the stockade, the unleafed orchard looks as if it were trying to root itself in the darkening sky.

• • •

"Why do they welcome him and listen to his talk?" A'onote asks Gaianniana, when they are settled in the sleeping closet away from the rest of the family. "Even my father's friend Rowahokon seems to accept Arosen. Does Rowahokon forget how Arosen's people at Canajoharie Castle dealt with him? Every time I notice Rowahokon's limp and those fingers missing from his right hand, I think how the Great Peace was broken when our southern brothers did that to him. He says they would have killed him if he hadn't escaped."

Gaianniana looks at her closely before answering. "That may or may not be," she says, "and it was a long time ago. You and I weren't even born yet, and he was not much more than a boy. He should not have been with the men, but it was a brave escape he made. It won him honor. Still, it was our people who attacked first."

This is news to A'onote. "Why did we?"

"In those days, the French had more power over us. Kahnawake was still a new settlement. Our people often did their bidding. That attack is one of the reasons we have tried to keep peace among the nations ever since. Our people saw what they had done to the Peace after that incident." Gaianniana looks at her closely again. "I don't understand why you bring this old matter up. Arosen is my cousin. And one of the Canienga people, even if he comes from the south. You always liked him"

"I do, but he seems to push us into war. I still don't understand why Atironta and Asientie, and even Rowahokon want to listen to him."

"Rowahokon welcomes Arosen because he would like to spare others. Arosen was just a child when all that happened. He has come to try to bring the people together. It is not right that our people are divided between the English and the French."

"So. He would turn us toward the English when we are sur-rounded by the French?"

"My father says Arosen does not care about the French or the English, and we should not either. He cares only for the Five Nations and what is good for the people. It looks as if maybe the English will drive the French away. I pay attention, and so should you. I expect to be part of the Women's Council when I am older. It is better to think about what is good for all the Canienga people."

Suddenly Gaianniana's serious look dissolves into a smile. "My cousin is very handsome. And he is Wolf Clan. Wolf can marry Turtle. Nice for you, my Turtle friend. I like him. If Wolf could marry Wolf, who knows? I might marry him myself."

. . .

The following night, the men, women, and children from several families tell stories around a roaring fire under a full white moon. Yet, even among friends, disagreement ripples like a current beneath a thin skin of ice on an autumn pond.

A'onote is gathering another ear of varicolored corn to be braided and dried for the winter, but she keeps an eye on Arosen across the circle, firelight flickering over his face. His name means "squirrel" she thinks, but he looks more like a wolf than a squirrel with his lean, proud bearing and almond eyes. His eyes remind her of Kenniontie's—keen and thoughtful. There is something in them that makes her want to seek them out. But there is also the thin white scar sunk into his cheekbone. How did he get such a wicked-looking scar? She wishes she had asked Gaianniana about it. Despite their talk, she still feels that his presence means trouble. Although Atironta likes him, he too seems wary of him. There is something quick and wily in his nature. Ever watchful he seems to A'onote. His eyes turn toward her and she looks down at her hands, deftly braiding the husks in the dancing light.

"He is looking your way!" says Gaianniana, laughing.

"I don't know what you are saying." A'onote gives a little snort of feigned disbelief. "He doesn't look at me. But I wish he would go away from us. He sows trouble like corn in the field. He should return to his people."

"We are his people, too, just like I told you yesterday." Gaianniana gets up. "I'm going over to talk to Desawennawen," she says, nodding toward a young man of the Turtle Clan and brushing the husks from her dress. "I'm sure he won't be as grouchy as you are. He always makes me laugh."

. . .

That night, voices invade her sleep. Moonlight falls through a crack in the wall that needs sealing and teases her awake. At first the voices are reassuring, speaking nonsense like the burbling of a small stream sliding through her mind. They twine together and flow on as if there is there is no single voice, just a gentle flow of sound to carry her. One voice breaks free of the murmuring and sounds clear.

". . . Montreal was ours in ancient times. The bonds that have held us together have been too loose to keep us strong today. Only by reaffirming your allegiance to the Five Nations and putting off the French can we hold our ground."

Asientie's voice comes forward, "Our ties with the French go very deep. A whole generation has now grown up with the Jesuits' teaching, and a new one is following. There are many who see the new religion as the only way to end the cycle of tribal warfare and revenge that plagued us after the Europeans came. Only two generations ago, Kahnawake was founded because the Great Peace was broken and people needed another way."

"But what are your own thoughts on the French religion, *Ak'sotha*?" This person addresses Asientie as grandmother, a term of honor when applied to any elder woman. "I say it with respect, but I don't think you hold to priests' teachings yourself. You must see how the alliance our Haudenosaunee fathers made with the English, sealed by the two-row wampum showing a river wide enough for both peoples, should be made even stronger now."

The young man's voice rises a little, and A'onote recognizes it as that of Arosen. His voice drives the gauze of sleep from her mind, and she listens tensely. He has business with the elders and has brought it to Asientie. A'onote reaches over to stroke Tsihon's head, and the dog sighs.

"I am old. I am not inclined to change my beliefs." In her mind, A'onote sees her grandmother's elegant gesture of rejection. "The covenant with the people beyond the sea has always been loose. Draw it tight and we will strangle ourselves. The English are too hungry and have never been known to bend with the wind."

"Listen to me, please! The French are weak. Allied with the French, the Kahnawake will loose everything!" His tone is urgent now, not appropriately respectful toward an elder of both the Women's Council and the Otter Society as it was just moments ago.

"It is not always wisest to ally oneself with the strongest. Your people at Canajoharie Castle have lost much ground in the south. Do you think the English will give you land north of the door if they take it? I think not."

"They promise us our ancestral lands and much in the West if we include them in a new covenant chain."

A'onote, wide awake now, stiffens and digs her hand into Tsihon's furry neck.

"And yet, we have not seen them give anything!" Asientie continues kindly. "I wonder if you will keep your river castles in the south. We prefer to honor the Great Peace as we have in the past. It is sacred because it leaves us free to keep our own counsel. It has lasted for this reason alone. The English have no place in this. The Five Nations will have to find another way to deal with them."

"But you would bring the French in?"

"You are a very young man. You have taken the counsel of a few to heart. I can see that your allegiance to the Five Nations is strong, but you would be wise to wait and watch and follow your own mind on these matters. Why do you come to bother an old woman? Perhaps you should be speaking to the chiefs."

"You know I have been speaking to Atironta and your sons, and to the war chiefs like Rowakohon too. Your chiefs disagree about how to align themselves."

"What I would urge on my chiefs is not what you look for. Now! It is true that we old ones sit and feed the fire, but I am tired. It is time for you to let an old woman alone."

A'onote hears a rustling as Arosen takes his leave. It is her grandmother's turn to sigh. A'onote would like to go and question her about the division among her people, but that is just what Arosen has done, and Asientie has said that she is tired.

. . .

As weeks go by, Arosen is seen frequently in the company of the younger chiefs, and less often with Atironta or Rowahokon. He remains friendly with Gaianniana's father and Tsiatekenha, Gentiyo's husband. Some of the elders look at him darkly and A'onote is glad of this. His presence makes her nervous.

"My mother says it does not matter whether the English are richer and more powerful. She says that they will do us no good in the long run, for they are hungrier for land than the French," says Gaianniana. "But my father agrees with Arosen that the French will be pushed out and we must think about what that means for us." The morning is cold, and there is frost on the ground. She and A'onote are setting out to harvest the hardiest of the winter squash.

A'onote whistles for Tsihon. She hates this talk of the English; they are rich, and they are powerful. She no longer wants to belong to any world they might own.

"Do you think Kahnawake will be divided?"

"Kahnawake *is* divided." Gaianniana drops her voice. "My father is away, and I haven't seen Arosen in days, but Gentiyo heard that he has asked some of our warriors to join the English in attacking the French in Montreal. I don't know if it's true."

A'onote looks up at the coppery leaves of a small beech tree at the edge of the field. Tsihon has caught a scent on the breeze and is crossing the browning garden in crazy zigzags, nose to the ground. A'onote watches her silently. The division of Kahnawake already seems like the end of the world to her. She can't imagine what a serious attack on Montreal would mean. Her world is about to be destroyed again.

. . .

Several weeks go by and there is still no attack on Montreal, but people look to Arosen. Why has he not returned to his people in the south?

Leaving the longhouse to visit Gentiyo one day, A'onote catches sight of Arosen heading toward her, a woven bag slung over his shoulder. Her first impulse is to look away and pretend not to see him, but he is heading straight for her. She hasn't seen him lately, and her feeling now is mostly confusion. If he is here, can it be true that he is working to help the English? She recovers herself and looks straight at him.

"You are still here, when so many have left," she says.

"You know that I always come to see you before I leave. I've brought you some game birds. Grouse mostly, small but very tasty."

"Thank you. I know how good they are. We will enjoy them." She is not sure what to say next. She is on her way out, but now there is this gift. Even more than this, she finds she wants to speak to him. "Would you like to come in and show Asientie what you've brought us?"

"You look as if you are on your way somewhere. If you wait, I'll leave these grouse with Asientie and walk with you. I would like that," says Arosen.

It seems as if he is gone a long time. Of course, he can't just drop the birds and go, she reminds herself. That is no way to behave when you bring a gift to an elder. He will have to sit for a time and talk. She calls Tsihon and sits on the rock in front of the longhouse petting her while she waits. She wonders why she didn't go in with him and realizes that she doesn't really want to see him with Asientie. She wants to walk and talk with him on her own.

"You didn't say why you are still here," she says when they finally begin walking toward Gentiyo's house. "Gaianniana heard that you have been trying to convince our men to join with the English in an attack on Montreal. She always claims that you are one of us, so this surprises me."

"You should ask me, if you hear things about me. So should Gaianniana."

"I am asking you now. Everyone is worried about this attack. I didn't ask anyone else, because I don't like to spread rumors. There are so many."

"But you wouldn't have asked me if I hadn't come to you." He looks tense, and for the first time, it seems to A'onote that Arosen is as worried as she is. "No one who was here at Kahnawake has gone to join the English, and I don't plan to join them either. My heart is not with the English or the French, it is with the Great Peace and the Canienga. I do not want to see our people divided." Arosen pauses. "Do you still have the flint I gave you after your adoption ceremony, the turtle I shaped by knapping in the old way?"

"I keep it with me in my bag." She draws it out of a quillwork bag tied at her waist, where once she kept the silver cup. "It's so pretty and sleek, and useful for so many things." A'onote looks down at her moccasins. "Also, I knew what you meant when you gave it to me, that I am Canienga, a person of the flint. It was the nicest of the presents." They are drawing close to Gentiyo's house.

"I am going south again," says Arosen. "I told Asientie this. I don't think the English will succeed in attacking Montreal this year, and I think it would be good for me to be away and let people talk. I hope you'll say good things about me and welcome me when I come back. I know you are of two minds."

A'onote can't say that she is not. She leans his way now that she is talking to him, but at other times she leans away. He places his hands on her shoulders. "I won't trouble Gentiyo by coming in with you. You'll be dancing with the women in the Green Corn Festival in the summer. I'll be there to see you."

CHAPTER 18

"I will turn fifteen before the Harvest Moon. And Gaianniana is dancing. It seems to me that I should dance when she does. We have always done things together."

"But you only have fourteen winters now. You know this is how we count," answers Kenniontie. She smiles. "The summers are easy. It is the winters that season a person. Your turn will come next year. Besides, there are more medicines you should master before you dance or you will not be ready to join the Otter Society when the time comes."

A'onote and Kenniontie are planting seeds into the mounds. Spring beauties, tiny white flowers with tracings of pink on the petals, carpet the ground around them, their crisp roots a source of food that, like the wild strawberries, requires no cultivation. This conversation has continued on and off for the past two moons, since A'onote learned that her parents would not let her dance this year. She had always assumed she would dance with Gaianniana.

"Gaianniana says there is no hard and fast rule, that you could let me dance if you wished to."

"She is right. The rule has to do with the wisdom of the elders. Even Gaianniana could have been prevented from dancing this year, if it had been decided so. But she is ready. It is still the exception for a girl to dance early. We are not ready to make that exception. As I say, you have much to learn, and you are still a girl."

"And Gaia is not?"

"I didn't say that. The ceremony itself has meaning. Gaianniana is a girl, but she is ready to move into womanhood. You are not, A'onote. You do not fully know your own heart. I would like to end this discussion now. We have tossed this back and forth long enough. It is settled now."

A'onote knows that it is settled, but it is still hard to accept. Hadn't she told Gentiyo, Rowahokon, Achiendase, even Ohnwatsihon, that she would be dancing? And Arosen, who will return for the ceremony, is expecting to see her dance. She feels it as a punishment to be left behind, although her parents and Asientie have made it clear that it is not meant as one. They had not realized that she expected to dance with Gaianniana, but they will not bend.

• • •

The strawberries have ripened and gone, the blueberries are picked over, the beans have climbed the corn stalks while the squash blossomed, and now the corn is green, ready for the early harvest. Although A'onote has been busy, both with planting and learning the uses of different plants and roots for medicines of the Otter Society, which she enjoys, the summer has dragged on. She has been to Montreal and bought ribbons, giving them to Gaianiana for her fancy dress. It is emerald green like the tunic she wore when A'onote first met her, Gaianniana's color. But the fabric is much finer this time and its decoration more elaborate. Now Kahnawake is alive with flutes and drums again for the Green Corn Festival.

"The ribbons you gave Gaia are so pretty," Gentiyo says. "It was generous of you to give away such lovely ones. I know it must be hard for you to watch her dance, when you are still waiting. You'll be all the happier for waiting when you finally join in."

"That's what my parents say. It may be true, but it doesn't feel that way now."

A'onote sighs. "I felt ashamed when I saw Arosen. I told him would be dancing when he was here for maple sugaring, and he said he would come, and here I am leading the children, just as I did last year."

"I doubt Arosen cares about that. He likes to spend time here, and he likes you, A'onote. He may hang back a little, because you are young and he does not want to offend your parents—especially if he is serious about you." A'onote shrugs, but Gentiyo goes on. "I think your parents are right that you don't really know what you want yet. Once you dance, you must be ready to make decisions. Not that you have to marry right away, but you have to know your mind. You haven't even decided whether to join in the communion at Mass."

"That is what my mother and Asientie say."

"I also think your parents have their own ideas about who you should marry when the time comes."

"What do you mean?" A'onote is startled. "You chose your own husband. They can't choose for me."

"No. I'm sure they would not, but they may want you to give Rowahokon a chance. He has achieved a lot for a young chief, and he is a friend of your family."

"Anyway, I don't want to think about marrying yet. Sometimes I still think of Joseph."

"There you are. Dancing doesn't mean that must marry soon, but once you have danced, the young men will give you reason to think about it. Hasn't Kenniontie told you this?" Gentiyo is smoothing her fancy dress.

A'onote sighs again. "Sometimes I feel I have no place among the children or the adults."

"Yes. I used to feel that way too, but you will see, you are becoming more and more yourself. That is what is needed for the dance."

Looking up, they see Arosen coming toward them in his fancy tunic with the yellow stripes.

"I'm glad I've found you," he says. "I thought we could watch the dancing together, A'onote. I'll just join it at the end and keep you company until then, if you'd like."

Gentiyo gives A'onote a meaningful look as Rowahokon approaches from the other direction. He greets them and passes them by, but A'onote wonders if he had planned to keep her company.

The drumming, the shaking of rattles, the chanting grows louder, and all of Kahnawake is heading for the central circle, where once again the men and women will take their places, moving in the circles that run in opposite directions so that the men and women pass each other as they dance. A'onote feels lighter after her conversation with Gentiyo and glad to have Arosen with her to watch Gaianniana dance, but he is heading west to do some trading in Seneca country the next day, before the end of the festival.

"I'm sure it was hard for you not to dance," he says that night, "but the rest of the festival will be the same as ever. Your friends will be with you. And I'll be back, as always." She knows now that she will be glad to see him when he returns.

• • •

As fall approaches, harvesting the late summer crops keeps A'onote and the other women busy. They can hardly keep up with the bounty of the rich land along the rapids.

Arosen does not return for the Harvest Festival that fall and neither does Joseph Kellogg. And just as A'onote feared, Gaia does seem to be leaving her behind since she danced with the women.

A'onote is grinding cornmeal from the dried corn outside Asientie's longhouse one day when Gaianniana stops by to see her.

"Gaia, you are spending more and more time with Desawennawen, almost as much as Gentiyo spent with Tsiatekenha before they decided to get married. You hardly have time for me these days," A'onote scolds, only half joking, as she greets her.

"I don't spend that much time with him at all!" answers Gaianniana. "I'm here with you now."

"You know what I mean. You seem to like him as much as he likes you. I don't see you flirting with others, the way Gentiyo did before she settled on Tsiatekenha. And I don't see as much of you. I suppose you've kissed him by now? Do you like it?"

Gaianniana smiles, the single dimple in her cheek appearing. "You will see. You're not so far behind me, A'onote. And I can already tell you who your suitors will be."

"But is Desawennawen the only boy who interests you?"

"It could be," answers Gaianniana. "It is like that sometimes.

He is funny and always finds little ways to make me happy, but he is also wise about many things."

They trade some gossip as A'onote grinds the corn. A'onote wonders if knowing her mind this way is what meant Gaianniana was ready to dance. Her mind turns to Arosen, and she wonders if it could be like that for her.

CHAPTER 19

The Very Cold Moon arrives, the dead of winter. Like many of the people of Kahnawake, Atironta and Kennionite are off at a hunting camp, leaving A'onote to stay and keep Asientie company. Though the time for maple sugaring is still far off, A'onote is putting the finishing touches on the birch sap buckets and the odd-shaped boxes they make for the maple sugar. Well into her fifteenth winter now, she looks forward to setting out for the maple groves— and further ahead to the Green Corn Festival, when she hopes to dance with the women at last.

Just outside the longhouse, she hears cheerful voices and a stamping of feet to shake the snow off, then Gaianniana is at the door with her mother, greeting them all. After the usual courteous questions, observations, and offerings of food, Gaia looks down for a moment, then up to Asientie, then to A'onote, her dimple appearing as she smiles.

"I have happy news that will not come as a big surprise," she says. "Desawennawen and I are going to the Council of Chiefs for permission to be married."

The other women cluster around her, but A'onote, stunned, is the last to join them. They have talked a great deal about this new development in Gaianniana's life, but she had somehow not seen this coming, not so soon, and she feels a little betrayed not to have heard it first. Surely Gaianniana should have come to her. The women put aside their work and bring out bread and the last of the previous year's sugar to be passed around.

"What kind of a wedding will you have?" asks Asientie.

"We both want to marry in the traditional Canienga way, Asientie. We will have a longhouse wedding in the Council House, when the chiefs approve it."

"Which I'm sure we will do," says Asientie. "You have chosen a fine young man. Just right for you, Gaianniana. You will both do well. I wish you great happiness."

After a few more minutes of talk, A'onote turns to Gaianniana. "Let's take Tsihon for a walk."

"I'm happy for you Gaia," she says as they emerge onto a path laced with melting ice. "Still, I wish you had told me before now. Do you really feel ready to marry? It is such a big step."

"You noticed yourself that I had no trouble making up my mind. We've known each other since we were children. I think we both knew before I danced with the women, even without talking about it."

A'onote is taken aback. "I've always known that you liked him, but you never said that when we talked back then."

"It was as if it had been understood so long, I didn't think about it. But once you know, you know. That was true for Gentiyo too. She might have known deep down, even while she flirted with Rowahokon. Once she made up her mind, there was no question. It may be another year or even more for you, but it will be the same. You'll know."

"I suppose Achiendase will be disappointed that you're having a traditional Canienga wedding."

"Achiendase has known for a long time that both Desawennawen and I are more comfortable with our traditional ways. My mother is disappointed that I will not be baptized, but both my parents are happy with my choice of a husband. And Asientie will like the old ceremony."

"Yes, she will," says A'onote. "I'm not sure I will be able to please her that way."

"Like my mother, she'll care more about who you marry than which ceremony you choose."

• • •

When Gaianniana's marriage is approved by the Chief's Council, they set a wedding date just before the Midwinter Festival. Ohosera, as a Wolf Clan chief and Gaianniana's mother's brother, is to give the welcoming speech and conduct the ceremony. A'onote dresses in her most elaborately beaded tunic and arrives at the council house with her family to find the couple seated on the central bench, each with a basket holding traditional items to symbolize their vows. Gaianniana's basket is filled with needlework and small tools to show how she will care for the family, and Desawennawen's holds the marriage bread to show his commitment to sustaining their new family. Their mothers sit on either side of them. A'onote gives a small wave to Gentiyo, who is a cousin of Gaia's new husband and, like him, a member of the Bear Clan.

After giving the welcoming speech, Ohosera addresses questions about this new commitment, first to each of the mothers, then to the bride and groom. Finally, the two stand and turn to each other to exchange their baskets, and the wampum that seals their marriage is passed for all to see. As everyone congratulates Gaianniana and her new husband, her mother and father break the marriage bread and pass it among the guests.

After they have greeted the newlyweds, Gentiyo grabs A'onote's hands in hers. "I guess you'll be next," she laughs, "but who it will be and when, I wonder."

"A'onote has plenty of time. She is in no rush to marry." Kenniontie sounds imperious, as if she wants to put an end to the discussion, and this annoys A'onote. When she dances with the women, she will be as ready as anyone, and that is not so far off.

As the evening's dancing begins, A'onote feels bereft. How strange to have her two best friends married. It is very cold. Tomorrow there will be games of snow snakes and canoe races on the open water to celebrate the Midwinter Festival. Once again, Arosen has not returned for an important event. And the Midwinter Festival always reminds her of Joseph Kellogg, who used to show up for it every year. It has been a long time since he has come.

• • •

As maple sugaring time approaches, Atironta's friend Rowahokon is a frequent visitor to the longhouse. The two have returned from a trip to the Seneca territory, at the Western Door of Haudenosaunee country near Lake Ontario, where the senior chiefs of the Five Nations met to confer over developments in the war. The Haudenosaunee with their various tribes, clans, and religions have been able to agree only to try to keep the peace among themselves and to hold to whatever other alliances they find convenient, but most are allied with the English.

Rowahokon has been named a peace chief, a new honor, especially since he is, at twenty-five, the youngest of them. A'onote notices his polite attention, and Kenniontie and Atironta seem to approve. A'onote remembers how quickly Kenniontie cut off any talk of marriage after Gaianniana's wedding and is not sure what to make of this seeming encouragement. It is a little warmer and, tired of winter, they have built a fire outside the longhouse. The two men will head out again to one of the hunting and fishing camps early the next morning, and Kenniontie, Asientie, and Ohnwatsihon will join them, leaving A'onote to keep Asientie company, but it is nice to have this break in the quiet of the winter.

"Tell me," Ohnwatsihon asks the men. "Who did you meet at the Western Door? Did anyone know anything about Joseph Kellogg?" Nearly eleven now, he is still in the grip of his fascination with Joseph's travels.

"We didn't see him," answers Rowahokon, "but I met with an Onondaga chief who saw him a year ago. He had been farther west than any of the rest of us. As far as the Mississippi, the great river our people crossed in ancient times before settling here."

"I wonder why he doesn't visit us anymore, especially with his sister here," A'onote wonders. "Of course, the Mississippi must be a long ways away."

Rowahokon looks questioningly at Atironta, who nods at him.

"After exploring the Mississippi with a Huron friend and one of the French voyageurs, they met up with a group of Englishmen who convinced him to travel with them as an interpreter. He went with them, and some say he is living among the English again."

A'onote looks up at the sky. A wisp of cloud floats across the gibbous moon that looks, she thinks, like a pumpkin that has lain too long on one side. Joseph too is gone, she thinks.

. . .

The next day in the chapel, A'onote watches Achiendase raise the host above his head. The host is encircled by the gold rays of a reliquary made at the court of the French Sun King. How strange, thinks A'onote, that the emblem for this French king, the sun, is the same as that of the Canienga creator, and it encircles the host too. She goes to Mass regularly and sometimes says her *rosaire*, but still she hangs back from being baptized and taking a new Christian name.

Suddenly, as those who have taken communion file past, Arosen is beside her. She is so surprised that she hardly takes in that he is now a communicant, and he has passed by her bench before she knows it. When the Mass ends, he is nowhere in sight. She wonders if he saw her there at all.

Throughout the day, she finds herself thinking of him as she goes about her business, weaving a fresh mat for the house, embroidering some fancy quillwork on a pair of moccasins her father sewed for her, sitting with Asientie, who is helping her to identify the dried plants she shows her. Each sound outside the house seems to be Arosen arriving. She doesn't ask Asientie, who would surely know about it. She doesn't really want to share her interest with anyone. When he hasn't come by evening, A'onote casts about for a reason to visit Gaianniana's house the next day. With so many people off at the hunting camps, she isn't sure who else might be there. How could Asientie fail to mention such interesting gossip?

The next morning her grandmother sits feeding the fire, looking into it as if it could tell her a story. A'onote opens the carved chest and takes from it a beaver coat edged with beads at the collar and closure.

"Asientie, there is firewood at a blowdown up the river. I am going to take Tsihon and a sled."

Asientie looks up at her. "That is a beautiful coat you wear to gather firewood. Be careful not to break the beadwork with your labor. Your mother spent a long winter working those beads." She gazes at her appraisingly. "Perhaps you will take someone with you."

"I thought I would see who is at Gaianniana's house. I think they may need firewood too."

"You look very pretty in that coat." Asientie looks up at the blue sky encircled by the smoke hole. "It is a beautiful day. Do not be too long."

A'onote takes a sled from the side of the longhouse and whistles for Tsihon, who rises from her place by the sleeping closet, stretching and bowing a little stiffly, but ready as ever for adventure. They head first for Gaianniana's house to see who might come with them. A'onote has seen none of Gaianniana's relatives during the past month and cannot remember whether any of them had been with Arosen in the chapel. She is surprised when it is her uncle, Onwekowa, who greets her, clapping her firmly on the shoulders.

"You honor us! Come and sit. Arosen is here. He joined us at the winter camp some time ago and persuaded me to come back to the village with him."

"I know Arosen," she answers, looking into the interior of the house.

Arosen rises from his place by the hearth fire. For a moment A'onote feels caught out, as if she had come with no other thought than to see him. It must be apparent in her hesitation.

"I'm glad to see you sooner than I expected, A'onote. I was

going to visit you and Asientie today. You once asked me whether I liked Kahnawake or the southern castles best. I have decided to settle at Kahnawake when summer comes."

"I thought I saw you taking communion at Mass the other day. I didn't know you were baptized."

"I was baptized by a missionary to the Seneca during the winter and took the Christian name François."

They sit by the fire and pass the pipe. Finally, Onwekowa turns to A'onote and smiles encouragingly. "You must tell us what has brought you here. Surely it is not only to welcome Arosen?"

"I am going for firewood, and I was hoping someone would come and help me get it home," she answers, and Arosen is immediately on his feet looking ready to go.

Back in the bright afternoon sun, A'onote and Arosen load firewood from an area of blown-down trees, which seems farther from the village than A'onote remembered. Tsihon and two other dogs poke around in the nearby woods. A'onote and Arosen are quiet at first as they pick their way through the tangle of downed trees.

"It was a good idea to come here. This will let us feed the fire for the rest of the winter. I wonder that it hasn't been more used before now."

"I don't think many people come up this way. The trail leads around it to a higher place. I've come here to swim in the summer." She drops an armload of wood onto the sled. "There is a pool with a smooth rock slide into this one. I often take Ohnwatsihon. The pool was very good this year, wide and deep, but the beach was covered by our firewood."

"It will be like rolling thunder when the snow melts after the Sugar Moon. Have you been here when the river breaks?"

"My father brought me once when I was very young. I could

hear it from the village. I thought it was gunfire. I haven't been back for the break-up since."

"Perhaps we will come for it together this year." Arosen carries an ash log to the sled, dusting the snow off his gloves after he drops it. "This will burn well." He looks at her, his dark head angled down like a cockaded bird. He is handsome but slight compared to many of the Kahnawake men. "I'm glad that you came looking for firewood. You were still of two minds when I was here before."

She flushes slightly and lifts her chin. "There was reason enough to worry about people connected to the English. I think I am safer when the English and French are enemies. It is when they make peace that I am of interest to them."

"I know there is a powerful family who wants you returned to them."

"It has been years since they have come looking for me. I don't think they're serious. Kenniontie says the English have strange beliefs. They think getting me back would show that their religion is sound. It is not me they want."

"Do you remember them, the English family?" They are sitting on a fallen log. The sky has clouded over, and in the grayness the world seems quieter, the place more remote than it did in the earlier brightness.

"I remember small things. My mother had red hair, like a fox, and there was a woman, a slave, who was good to me. I had brothers and a sister. I remember them like shadows, except for my brother Stephen. My father beat him once with a cane. I think it was for running in a field and putting our younger brothers in danger. I was always a little afraid of my father, not for that, but because he was so stern about ordinary things. He wasn't patient and playful like Atironta."

"I've heard the English discipline their children by beating them. Our people almost never do." There is a pause as Arosen weighs his words. "But the scar on my cheek was given to me by my father before he left Canajoharie Castle, where my mother and brothers still live."

"How did he do that to you?"

"He was drunk. I had fourteen winters and was the first child in my family. My brothers don't remember my father as a noble man. I do, and it hurt me all the more to see him change. He took to drinking with the English soldiers when he had business with them. He tried many cures, but he could not give it up. It got worse. He cut my face when I tried to wrest a knife from him. I don't think he meant to. He dropped it when he saw what he had done. Soon after that he left."

A snowbird is picking in the snow at seeds from the blown-down trees. A'onote watches it for a moment, then looks directly at him, her gaze serious. "Did you ever see him again?"

"No. I don't know what happened to him. He never came back, and my mother finally married another man, a man of the Bear Clan like my father, but he was never the man my father was before the spirits."

"You must have admired your father. It sounds as if you loved him too."

"I did. I was glad for my mother and two young brothers that she married again, but since my grandparents died, I've spent less time there. I went back to Canajoharie when I left here a year ago to begin earning my title as a Pine Tree Chief. My mother's family had taken on the English faith. We've had to deal with them, but I am changing my mind about the English. I have come to trust them less than I did when I was last at Kahanawake. They are moving up the river like salmon to a spawning ground. That is one reason I am here. There will be nothing for us there."

"I saw my English father here once when I first arrived." A'onote's cheeks are bright with cold as she speaks. "It was as if I did not know him more than any other stranger, and he did not know me more than he would know Ohnwatsihon or Gaianniana." A'onote shivers, noticing that they have been sitting too long." Asientie will be expecting me. We should secure our sled and move along."

"The river runs one way. You are fortunate to be of a powerful family here." Arosen gives a loud whistle for the dogs and smiles. "I will have to prove myself in Kahnawake." As he secures the last tie on the sled he leans over, finding the edge of her mouth with his lips. He kisses her once more, gently, before turning away.

His kiss has plucked a string that vibrates at the center of her body. She steals another glance at him as they go. He looks resolute and inward as he pulls the sled, as if he has forgotten she is with him. She tries to read his expression, but he seems focused on something she cannot guess. A'onote feels as if she has just emerged from an icy pool, all the heat in her body sparkling to the surface.

. . .

When they reach the village, before A'onote has even considered whether she will ask him in, Arosen asks if he can come in and see Asientie. She has not been inclined to share this encounter with Asientie, but she assents. She feels, somewhat resentfully, that she has been pushed back into the role of a child who sits by while the adults conduct their business.

"Welcome," Asientie addresses Arosen. "You must sit with me and we will talk. This seat may be good for you after all. I thank you for helping my granddaughter with the wood. We are grateful for it."

A'onote notices that Asientie has let the fire grow bigger than is usual. Of course, she would have expected a guest after the wood gathering. It would only be polite for anyone who had helped to come in and visit. But had she guessed who it would be?

CHAPTER 20

"So," Ohnwatsihon teases. "Shall we bet on whether Arosen or Rowahokon will visit today? I have some plum pits ready as markers." Ohnwatsihon has returned from the hunting camp with Rowahokon and the women, while Atironta joined another group and may not return for weeks.

Arosen did not go back to the hunting camp with Onwekowa but has stayed in Kahnawake through the Sugar Moon and into the Fishing Moon, only making short trips to hunt and trap game and visiting Asientie's longhouse as often as he can. Rowahokon has also been stopping in frequently, and A'onote feels flattered but a little uneasy about his visits. She is always a little on edge with him.

"That's enough," says Sientiesie. "It's no business of yours, Ohnwatsihon. Anyway, we haven't seen either of them for several days." But as soon as Sientiesie has silenced Ohnwatsihon, Arosen appears as A'onote expected. They have planned to see if the ice at the waterfall is ready to break up and to do some fishing.

"Hey!" says Ohnwatsihon, and greetings are exchanged all around.

"Why don't you take Ohnwatsihon with you?" suggests Kenniontie when they tell her where they are going.

"I have other plans for Ohnwatsihon today," answers Sientiesie before anyone else can say a word. Ohnwatsihon looks disappointed, and A'onote notices Kenniontie shoot Sientiesie a look of annoyance.

The snow is beginning to melt, and they step out into a warm day, the air damp and foggy from the melting.

"I think your mother would like to get me out of Rowahokon's way."

"I think my mother has little to say in the matter, and I know she likes you," A'onote answers. But she knows that her mother prefers Rowahokon, who is a longtime friend and a Peace Chief as well.

"It is best that we conduct ourselves properly with your parents." Arosen looks thoughtful. "They consider you very young. It is not so long until the Green Corn Festival. I think I should do more traveling until then. It will give them time. And it will give you time too."

"I am not interested in Rowahokon."

"I'm glad to hear you say so, A'onote. I don't like to go away, but I think in a week I must. The festival is not so far away." But it seems very far away to A'onote. Arosen looks at her as if expecting her to urge him to stay, but A'onote isn't sure what she wants.

·　·　·

When she gets home with her string of fish, only Kenniontie is there, and A'onote finds she cannot follow Arosen's advice and let the matter lie.

"Why do you not want me to be with Arosen?" she asks. "I'm not interested in Rowahokon, and you seem to push him on me."

"I don't choose who comes to visit you, A'onote. I don't push anyone on you. You are young and you have not danced in the women's dance yet. There is good reason for that." Kenniontie is smoothing a new mat on the floor, pushing it into a corner with a long, high-arched foot, bending to flatten it with a graceful sweep of her strong hand. The early witch hazel has already bloomed, and the scent of its crushed flowers fills the house.

A'onote watches her mother's beautiful long fingers pluck a splinter that has lodged in her palm. "I will dance soon enough, at Green Corn time. Why would you keep me from him?"

"I will not keep you from him. You may have fifteen winters now, but you are still young. It is fine to flirt!" Kenniontie smiles. "But I think this is not the right time or the man for you to marry. He has no one here to bring the marriage bread. You are Asientie's granddaughter. Someone like Rowahokon would be more to my liking for you. I don't say that it must be him, but a man of his stature would be better. People have great regard for you. You walk Gannestenawi's path, and I expect you will earn her name."

"Arosen is Gaianniana's cousin. Her father has great regard for him and so does mine."

"I do not think there is much to consider here yet, since you are not ready to marry. Your father and I feel you are young and un-settled, you have much to learn before you can be even a junior member of the Otter Society, and Achiendase does not think you should marry yet either. Onnontio does not wish it."

A'onote's head comes up sharply. "Onnontio! Why would Gov-ernor Vaudreuil concern himself with my marriage?"

Kenniontie speaks soothingly. "Onnontio has nothing to do

with your marriage. It is only that he wants to arrange a visit with the Dutch messenger this summer. Everyone is tired of this long war. We must show good will. It will not hurt to meet. It furthers the hope of peace." Kenniontie nods toward Asientie's carved chest, which the two of them lift onto the new mat.

A'onote looks accusingly at her mother. "So this has nothing to do with my marriage. I could meet with them, married or not. It is not to my liking, but I have done it before."

"I shouldn't have mentioned it. But they would take it as an insult if you were to be married before they spoke to you, as if we had been dishonest and arranged a marriage to keep you here."

A'onote shrugs. "What is the weight of it if they think ill of us? Why pretend that the door is open when it is not? I am tired of being a marker in someone else's game." Her face flushes and the words come fast, accusingly.

"If I thought you were ready and Arosen was right for you, if Atironta and Asientie thought it too, perhaps I would not worry about the game. I would put all my seeds with Arosen and say that you had chosen and we agreed. But even Gaianniana's family can't truly vouch for Arosen. Her mother left Arosen's grandmother's house a very long time ago."

"And so did Arosen."

"Not so very long ago. No one knows for sure where his loyalty lies. I do not want to hear any more of this matter now." Kenniontie gives a cursory glance around the room before going out.

• • •

Walking by the stream with her a few days later, Arosen asks A'onote about the visit. "Do you think you would ever be tempted to return with the Dutch trader?" he asks.

"Why would I leave here with a stranger?" She stops and looks seriously at him. "Even if you were nowhere in my life, I would not return with this man who comes for me. If this man can come so far, why can't the Reverend Williams? Atironta or Kenniontie would have long since come had I been taken from them. You would come." A'onote shoots him a dark look. "I wish you weren't leaving."

She plucks a budding leaf from a tree and turns away. "I am in the middle of everything, not one thing or another, and I don't think I can carry on like this much longer. I am not child or woman, though I have lived fifteen winters now, and my family has not even said for certain that I will dance with the women this year. I think Kenniontie is afraid that she will lose me if I marry you." A'onote peels the pale green bud with her thumbs as she speaks. "This summer, a man who is nothing to me will come and try to get me to leave here. It may be a man I have seen before, or it may be a different one. It doesn't matter. When he comes I know exactly how important I am. And Kenniontie and Atironta will stand by, and let this happen. Does anyone know what this man's interest is? Why should they insist that I see him? If I have a father in Guerrefille, let him come for me. I have no father but Atironta, because none acts like a father to me. This is a game they all play with me. If you play it too, this is the end. They all want me in the middle, unable to move."

A'onote pulls Arosen to her, burying her face in his neck and kissing him urgently.

"That is true," he answers quietly. "But this will change."

When Arosen leaves, Rowahokon continues visiting, but he too has business away from Kahnawake and does not come often. A'onote is relieved. She could send him away if he declared his feelings, but he has not. It is planting time, and she spends much of her time in the fields now, laughing and talking with the women. In the evenings, she works on her fancy dress. She is determined to win the right to dance with the women. She will be ready when the time comes. So far, they have heard nothing of the Dutch trader.

CHAPTER 21

When Onnontio's petition finally arrives early in the summer, a moon before the Green Corn Festival, it is Achiendase who tells her. He stops her in the chapel after Mass one day to say that her brother Samuel Williams is heading for Montreal and has asked to see her.

"Samuel Williams." She finds she can't picture him and feels only stunned at the thought. "I suppose I must see him? I don't know who he is to me now or what it means that he is my brother." But deep down, she feels so shaken that it must have meaning. After seven years, someone from her English family has come to see her.

"He will be here within a few days." Achiendase speaks gently. "That gives you time to think about it. Of course, Governor Vaudreuil, Onnontio, will want you to see him, but it is up to you, A'onote. I can only imagine how strange it is to have one of your English family come after all these years, when you have made a life here. It is many years since I have seen my own family in France."

He looks closely at her, and A'onote realizes that she has never thought about where he came from. "I came here as a very young priest, not so much older than you are now."

"Have you ever been back?"

"No. I am settled here for life, and my brother there cannot imagine the world I live in."

"You would see your brother if he came, I think."

"I suppose I would, though he would be a stranger. And there would never be any question of his wanting me to return with him. We are both old now, and you are young—a whole life ahead of you." Achiendase pauses. "Of course, with so many French in Montreal, I still speak the same language as my brother."

"Does Kenniontie know about this?"

"I would have told you both if she had been at Mass this morning, but I thought it better to give you time to think about it than to wait," says Achiendase. "Have you given any thought to being baptized? I have not wanted to ask you too soon, but I see that you are becoming as devout as Marie Gentiyo. You come to Mass now almost as often. She entered the church just before she danced with the women and celebrated it all at once."

"It was a very happy time for her. I have looked forward to being baptized too, but something has held me back. I think I will know after I see my brother." She looks out the open door at the rising sun just striking path leading back to the longhouse.

"I have faith, A'onote. You will stay in Kahnawake with your people and will find your way into the church. Say your beads tonight. It will give you strength. But I won't give Onnontio an answer until I see you again. Bless you, child," says Achiendase as A'onote heads out into the barely dawning day.

The early light is so pretty that it makes her sad for some reason. Achiendase has said she has time to consider whether she will see her brother. She doesn't see how she could refuse.

Kenniontie and Asientie look very surprised when she tells them. "I hadn't thought there would be Englishmen coming now, after planning the attack on Montreal, then taking Port Royal, and still no peace in sight." Kenniontie looks lost in thought for a moment. "You have said you will see him, and Atironta and I will stand with you on that. But how do you feel about it after all this time?"

"I feel only that I should do as you have taught me and welcome a member of my family, who has done me no harm. I know he will be a stranger to me, but I am curious too." She suddenly realizes that this is true, and a weight feels lifted from her.

"It's no surprise that you would be curious," says Asientie. "The surprise is that he's here. Well, we will stand together when he comes. We have nothing to fear from him."

But A'onote's feelings continue to swing between two poles. Why now? she wonders. And if he can come now, why not before? Tsihon whines in her sleep and her feet move as if she were chasing a rabbit. She settles next to the dog, rests her cheek against a shoulder for a moment, and runs her hand over the thick fur at her neck.

The next day, Achiendase stops by to tell her that Samuel Williams is in Montreal. "He would like to come to Kahnawake in two days. You have given it more thought?" he asks. A'onote realizes he no longer wears his hat during the summer, and his skin has grown darker. Except for his short, grizzled beard and long hair pulled back with a ribbon, he could be one of the Kahnawake men. I have become one of the Kahnawake people too, she thinks, and wonders what her brother Samuel will think of her.

"I will see him," she replies.

. . .

When A'onote returns from Mass with Kenniontie the next morning, the sun has not yet topped the horizon, the plum trees only spectral shapes against the predawn sky. Yet Arosen sits in front of the longhouse deep in conversation with Atironta and Asientie. He rises to greet the women and places both hands on A'onote's shoulders. "I have come back early. I wanted to see you before I go to visit the Western Door. We are finished talking, and I am ready to take a walk. Will you come with me, A'onote?" She notices Asientie give Kenniontie a warning look.

"Yes, I would like that," she answers.

Arosen says nothing as they set out. The horizon is like a striped trade blanket, a thin margin of plum diffusing into a band of robin's-egg blue. One star hangs like a beacon in the blue. They head toward the spot among the cedars that Gaianniana showed her so many years ago when she was a little girl newly arrived in a foreign world.

"I hadn't expected to see you until the Green Corn Festival. I'm glad you've come. What brings you back?" They have just hit the narrow trail that leads to the higher ground, and Arosen seems reluctant to speak.

"You know, there has been more trouble in the English colonies," Arosen begins as they pass through the thicket and enter the little clearing among the tall cedars.

"The war goes on," she answers quietly. To A'onote, this seems a strange conversation to be having when they've been apart for weeks. Isn't he even interested in her visitor? She is sure Kenniontie has told him.

"Yes, it goes on," he says. He looks to her a little weary. "I heard from the scouts that your brother was coming up this way. And it seemed to me that I should talk to you before you see him. I heard other news about him as well, more troubling."

"He has become a soldier rather than a minister like my English father?" A'onote looks up into the feathery canopy of the cedars and breathes their dry, familiar fragrance. The star is still visible, though it grows smaller as the blue grows brighter.

"A'onote, if it were just that . . ." Arosen pauses. "It is worse."

"What is it then?" She looks at him warily.

"In the spring, early in the Planting Moon, thirty men attacked a small group of Abenaki people, peaceful traders going about their business on the Connecticut River unarmed—women and children among them."

"Yes, it was a terrible thing. They killed them all. We all heard about it." But she is already afraid of what comes next. The Abenaki are the people who had taken Stephen, but he had been traded away years ago.

"Your brother Samuel Williams led that attack, A'onote. He has come for you, but he also comes to Governor Vaudreuil as a representative of the English Governor Dudley to trade for prisoners." Arosen pauses again as she takes this in. "I'm sorry, A'onote."

"Some in the party sold the Abenaki people's scalps for bounty," she says quietly.

"Some of them did." She finds herself remembering the wolf's head nailed to the meetinghouse door in Guerrefille, but it is the chapel in Kahnawake she sees, where such a thing could never happen.

"And how did you hear that Samuel Williams led them?"

"I didn't come until I had heard it from many sources—Indian, English, Dutch. Everyone seemed to know it." Arosen shakes his head. "Vaudreuil, Onnontio, must know it too."

A terrible thought strikes her. "Were other members of the Williams family involved?"

"No. I asked about them. I found some happier news for you, too. Your brother Eleazer has become a minister, and Stephen Williams is studying in Boston to become one too. They are not known as warlike men, though English ministers sometimes are."

"Thank you for finding that out. I will never meet with Samuel Williams now. Will you come with me to tell Achiendase? We will let him know that we mean to be married too. I know he can smooth the path." A'onote begins to reach for Arosen's hand, but he pulls her into his arms and kisses her.

"We'll both be ready when I come back from the Western Door," he says.

A'onote wonders only briefly what he means. As they walk along, she feels a calm, steely anger return. "I see that the English are as dishonorable as people say they are. And Onnontio, Vaudreuil as you call him, is not much better," she says.

The morning star shrinks to a needle's point as they head toward the little wood that separates the mission from the village of Kahnawake. Fallen plum petals are browning, fading back into the earth beneath her feet. In addition to this cold anger, she is suffused with shame. She has been separated from her English family in time and space, in habit and religion, but never before in common humanity. Never has she heard or felt that any of her English family was monstrous. No matter what the English army did, it had not seemed to touch her family.

There was a brook, she thinks, near Guerrefille, where English men were massacred as they stopped to pick berries on their way to deliver goods to the nearby town. Bloody Brook it was called, after that. The name caught her imagination when she was young. She remembers the story of how the Wampanoag chief known as King Philip had led the attack on the men. According to the Reverend Williams, they had been tempted by the Devil's grapes and found wanting. These men were held up as an example of what happens to those who fail to be vigilant. Vigilant in all things, A'onote remembers now, especially in regard to temptation. That is what the children were to remember when they strayed from their labors. But her brother Samuel has been found wanting in a worse way.

She remembers how shamed she felt by her tree-of-peace tunic and reddened cheeks in the mission when she saw her father there all those years ago. Her father's look made her feel as if she had become something he didn't recognize, something he did not want to recognize, though she had done nothing wrong.

It seems to A'onote that the voice that has spoken to her ever since she was a child has grown stronger as it merged with a gift from Gannestenawi. It has never led her astray.

Now the voice within her tells her that she does not have to be ashamed of her connection to a man who killed innocent people for a bounty. Kahnawake has been a refuge for many whose people have done terrible things, even to the people of Kahnawake themselves. But it hurts to refuse her brother. In spite of everything, he is the first person from her early life that she might have seen after so many years. She desperately wishes the horror undone. She cannot bear to think of him, and, if he could kill those people for bounty, what would he think of her?

• • •

Achiendase is sitting outside under a tree in front of his house next to the mission when they catch sight of him. He dries the tip of his pen and rises.

"A'onote! François Arosen! Welcome. I heard that you had returned." Achiendase's voice sounds heartier than usual, as if he is forcing it, thinks A'onote. "Let us sit in the sun and talk. The mission is dark and cold today. I have been writing to my superior about the goings on here and am glad enough for a break."

"Arosen has brought news about my brother Samuel Williams," says A'onote. "I no longer want to meet him, so we thought we should come right away."

"I can easily send one of the younger priests with your message. But I would like to know what made you change your mind." A'onote looks to Arosen, her jaw clenched. She can hardly stand the thought of repeating what she has heard, so Arosen tells the story for her.

"I'm sorry, child," he says after hearing it. "Onnontio should not have asked you to see him. I believe he must have known. He doesn't share everything with us poor Jesuits. Our relations are strained."

"If he knew, he doesn't deserve to be called by that honorable title. I will call him only Vaudreuil, as Arosen does. But we have other matters to consult you about, Achiendase. Samuel Williams counts for nothing now and neither does Vaudreuil. There are two matters I would like to discuss. One is easy, the other harder."

"Go on," says the priest.

"First, I would like to prepare to be baptized before the Green Corn Festival. I have decided. The voice is strong within me now, and this, I know, will please you."

She looks over at Arosen. "The next matter concerns us both, and you can probably guess it. Arosen, François Arosen, and I would like to be married in the chapel this year. My parents will not want us to marry so soon. If I am to marry, they would like me to marry someone already settled in Kahnawake."

"I am returning to take a seat at Kahnawake," says Arosen. "I was baptized among the Seneca, as you know. You say we learned little from the visit of our chiefs to England. But I have learned enough. In the end we will gain nothing from the English."

Achiendase turns to A'onote. "You must know that your mother has spoken to me. How can I go against her wishes?"

"Achiendase," A'onote replies. "We have come to speak to you about ourselves. We wish to marry in the chapel as members of the church. Not tomorrow, but this year. I believe that you could help us to change my parents' minds. I must be allowed to dance with the women this year, and I would like them to approve our marriage."

"Kenniontie feels that you are young," responds the priest. "And she objects to your haste in this decision. Arosen, you lack a long history in this community. Kennionite fears she will lose her daughter. What do you say to this?"

Arosen opens his mouth to defend himself, but A'onote is quicker.

"There is nothing hasty in this decision. We have known each other a long time. Everyone knows this, just as everyone knows that Arosen will remain here. Gaianniana's mother can bring the marriage bread. My mother knows this well. I have waited through the spring and into the summer. Arosen has stayed away. I will be baptized and dance with the women at the Green Corn Festival. I do not know what is wanted of me." A'onote looks down at her lap to quiet herself. She picks at the beads on one of her bright medallions. The unusual green and red beads remind her of the tree of peace that Kenniontie stitched onto her first tunic at Kahnawake, so many beads on that tunic, many of precious pink shell.

"I am glad to know you want to be baptized, A'onote." Achiendase pauses, looking from one of them to the other. "As for the marriage," he turns to Arosen, "I believe you are devout and will do well, François Arosen. You are a thoughtful man, and A'onote could not do better, as far as I am concerned." Before they can thank him, the priest continues. "It will be wisest to take things step by step. I am willing to discuss your marriage with Asientie and your parents, when the time comes. If you tell them you are ready to be baptized, they will surely let you dance with the women. I think your parents have been waiting for this, and perhaps Asientie has been too. Arosen has shown honor in coming now, instead of carrying on with his business when he heard news that mattered to you, but I would wait to mention marriage. Take one step at a time. A'onote, you will have to choose a baptismal name."

They rise, thank the priest, and head through the clearing for the sun-dappled wood beyond. "He is on our side," says Arosen. "And I think he is also right. I will go after you announce that you plan to be baptized. It will go more smoothly this way. You will dance, and we will go on from there."

They return to Asientie's longhouse together. Now Atironta is there with the women. He is working on a wooden whistle with his knife, while the women add beans and squash to a pot over the fire.

"We have been to Achiendase," says A'onote. "He will send one of the younger men to carry the message that I will not see Samuel Williams."

"This is for the best," says Atironta. "It was good of Arosen to come and tell us about him. It was a cruel business. I am sorry that it is so, A'onote."

"I spoke to Achiendase about something else too. I have asked to be prepared to be baptized before the Green Corn Festival." A'onote

"This is a great joy!" Kenniontie hugs her. "It is something one can only come to on one's own. I am very happy. This is a great day for us."

A'onote knows that she will dance with the women now, as long as she continues to do well with her lessons on healing.

The next morning, Arosen leaves for the Western Door. A'onote walks as far as the stockade gate with him before they embrace and part again. "I will be here to see you dance," Arosen promises her again, as he passes through the gate. "We have come a long way, you and I."

· · ·

Later in the day, when A'onote goes to look for Gaianniana, Desawennawen is outside the house he has built for them near Gaia's mother's. He greets A'onote formally and immediately turns and goes inside. Relations between a woman and the men related to her by marriage are always formal in the village, just as there is a prescribed formality between a woman and her son-in-law, though he might live in her house much of the time. A'onote has noticed how Asientie and Atironta treat each other. She waits outside the house for her cousin to appear.

"My husband said that you were here." Gaianniana looks sleepy. "I was waiting outside with him before, but I had something to attend to." She laughs. "He runs like a rabbit when you arrive! You must come to the hunting camp with us in the fall. Then you might know each other better."

"I don't know, Gaianniana. It may depend on what Asientie does." But A'onote would like to go. She has felt more distance between Gaianniana and herself since Gaia's marriage, and since she usually stays to help Asientie, she has rarely gone to the hunting camps. Things are more relaxed when the village breaks up and smaller groups disperse through the hunting territories. People let down their customary reserve. "If Asientie goes with Atironta and Kenniontie, I will go with you this year. I would like that. Otherwise I think I will stay with her. But I have news. It is certain now that I will dance with the women this year."

Gaianniana throws her arms around A'onote. "Ah, my friend! I was sure they would let you, but I have waited for this moment. Asientie has given me a special privilege for when you dance, but I want to save it for a surprise." Gaianniana hurries on. "Perhaps Arosen will come with us to the hunting camp. By then maybe

Kenniontie will be ready to accept the marriage bread. My mother would be proud to be the one to bring it to her."

"He will be back before then, but what my mother will do I can't say. I think she likes him a little better now." She looks over at Gaianniana hopefully. "We will take it step by step."

CHAPTER 22

A'onote settles on Marguerite as the saint's name for her baptism. It has a pretty sound and reminds her not only of the saint but of a young Frenchwoman who has a shop in Montreal where she likes to buy ribbons and fancy lace. The Green Corn Festival begins tomorrow, and Arosen has not yet arrived, but this doesn't worry her.

"I didn't expect him to be here for this ceremony," she tells Gentiyo before they go into the chapel. "He'll be here when I dance tomorrow." Her whole family is in the chapel, even Asientie and Gaianniana, who have not entered into the communion. Everyone is dressed in fancy dress for the special Mass. There are to be three people baptized, a very old woman named Aronhia, and a boy not much older than Ohnwatsihon, named Atongatekhon, and A'onote. They have prepared together during the past few weeks and know one another well now. Watching Achiendase raise the host in its splendid circle of gold flames, she thinks, "This is the last time I will watch the communicants file up to the rail without me."

When the communion ends, the three who have prepared to be baptized are called forward. A'onote is the first to repeat the creed she has memorized in the Canienga tongue. She feels Achiendase cross her forehead with cool water, and he places a thin round piece of bread like a moon on her tongue. When the others have done the same, there is a small festival of greetings, everyone congratulating the new communicants and trying out the names—Marguerite, Catherine, Peter. And she does feel something new within her that goes beyond the new name that some will use and others will not. With each name, she seems to become stronger and more herself. Tomorrow's ceremony will seal her place as a woman and the youngest member of the Women's Council, and tell her what name she has earned.

· · ·

The next day, she scans the gathering as flutes, water drums, and the shaking of rattles greet her approach to the central longhouse for the naming ceremony. And still she does not find Arosen. "He will be here for the dancing," she tells herself as her uncle addresses the assembly the way he did so many years ago, when she was named A'onote and adopted into her family and the Turtle Clan. Now her second naming ceremony begins, making her a full member of the Haudenosaunee League, part of the Great Peace, but she is distracted by a twinge of doubt as her uncle steps forward to speak.

"Now, you of our nation, be informed that A'onote Marguerite Gannestenawi has ceased forever to bear her birth nation's name and has buried it deep in the earth. Henceforth let no one of our nation mention the original name or nation of her birth as setting her apart from us."

Atironta and Kenniontie step up with the wampum that

records her new name, Gannestenawi, and they hand it to Asientie for safekeeping with the elders. Again, as he did many years ago, A'onote's uncle Onwekowa takes her by the arm and announces her name three times to the assembled clans, then sings a song of thanksgiving as the others chant.

As the chanting dies down, Gaianniana steps into the circle and takes her hand, lifting her head proudly to speak to the assembly. "It is a strong name, Gannestenawi, She Who Gathers in the Harvest. It is the name won by this sister of my heart. Marguerite Gannestenawi is indeed one who gathers in the harvest, one of our own."

A'onote realizes gratefully that the name Gannestenawi is given not only by her elders but by Gaianniana.

"I have something else for you," whispers Gaianniana urgently as people surge in to congratulate her. "Meet me at the cedars before the women's dance and I will give it to you."

Once Marguerite, as she tries to think of herself, has acknowledged all the greetings and congratulations, there is not much time before the women's dance. Despite her happiness at her new status, she keeps searching the assembly for Arosen, until it occurs to her that perhaps he is waiting at the cedars, and that this is why Gaianniana wants her to come there. She slips away as soon as she can.

But only Gaianniana is waiting for her there.

"Gaia, what you said at the naming was beautiful. It makes me doubly happy. This was the special gift, a gift to both of us."

"Marguerite Gannestenawi, I meant all I said. You are a sister of my heart," she pauses for a moment, "and my friend A'onote as well. I have news from Arosen. When he saw he would not be able to come to watch you dance, he sent a runner."

Marguerite's heart sinks, "How . . . ?"

Before she can finish her thought Gaianniana rushes on. "It is good news. You will see." She withdraws a silver bracelet from her pouch, wrought like no piece of silver Marguerite has ever seen. "He sent this for you. It came from far to the west, he said. Isn't it strange and beautiful?" She looks wonderingly at the silver bracelet's open curves, a little like Canienga woodcarving in its winding, openwork shape. She runs her fingers over the smooth, shining silver, wishing Arosen were here to give it to her himself. But she recognizes its significance. One doesn't come across such a gift every day. She feels sure he will come soon.

"I wonder who could have shaped this silver so beautifully," she muses. "Did the runner tell you when he'll come?"

"He only said it would be soon. He didn't say why he couldn't come or how soon it would be."

She is torn between happiness and missing Arosen.

"You know," says Gaianniana, "this will make it easier for you. This present will help your parents see his seriousness. They will not regret Rowahokon so much. Put your bracelet on. It is lovely, isn't it? I have never seen such work before."

Marguerite pushes up her sleeve and fits the bracelet just above her elbow. "It will be our secret, for today, anyway. I don't know how much difference this would make to my parents." But her hand keeps returning to the bracelet on her arm.

· · ·

As they head back for the central longhouse, where the women's dance will begin, she looks down at the fancy needlework on her dress, patterned like the downy woodpecker but with medallions of red, green, and blue scattered across the black and white pattern and all down her sleeves. It is as lovely as her original adoption dress, which Asientie has put away in her chest, and she is proud of her needlework, wishes Arosen could see it.

The women's dance begins, a slow counterclockwise shuffle, the women turning their bodies to the side as they dance, the men's chanting rising and falling around the dancing women. Asientie, Kenniontie, Sientiesie, Gentiyo, Gaianniana—she joins them now—along with all the rest of the women of Kahnawake. She is one of them.

After the sacred dances in the longhouse, there are other games, dances, and songs lasting far into the night. Later in the evening, she finds Kenniontie sitting next to one of the fires. She studies the fire, banked with stones and tended carefully because of the drought, then looks over at her mother.

Kenniontie smiles at her. "A'onote Marguerite Gannestenawi, you are tired. Such a beautiful day this has been. Your father and I are very proud. We will remember this day always."

"I will remember it too, and I thank you for it."

This does not seem like a moment to bring up Arosen. With a secret pleasure, Marguerite once again runs her hand up her loose, medallioned sleeve to where the silver bracelet hugs her arm. She is satisfied with this day and her passage. She turns to Kenniontie, brimming with a sleepy joy that she cannot fully share with her mother.

"I'm going back to the house to sleep. I will find my father and thank him too before I go. I am so happy to be among the women now."

"This will be the beginning of much happiness for you. I give thanks every time my eyes fall on you. We are blessed." The almond eyes hold hers, serious, at peace.

"We are blessed," she assents with a smile.

Their love for her on this night seems boundless, and it is shadowed only by her uncertainty about Arosen's whereabouts and whether her parents will accept him and bless them. She rises and leaves the fire to find her father and bid him good night.

. . .

"Marguerite Gannestenawi!"

As she enters a little avenue of fruit trees that separates the bonfire from her home, she hears her name and turns. Rowahokon approaches. Throughout the day she has glimpsed him among the dancers, occasionally catching his eye as they passed each other in the circle. Once, during the Fish Dance, where partners shift, she found herself dancing with him, and it made her uneasy. He is taller and more broadly built than Arosen, dressed elegantly in green-and-red-trimmed buckskin with a linen shirt beneath the tunic. She noticed that he danced easily, in spite of his slight limp. They spoke politely after the women's dance, Marguerite flushing, because this was the man Kenniontie and Atironta would choose for her. Rowahokon extends his arm now, placing his hand on her shoulder in congratulations.

"It is a great day, Marguerite Gannestenawi."

"It is a very happy day for me. I thank you."

Suddenly, like a diving bird, his mouth seeks hers and plants a swift, hard kiss, as if feeding it to her. Her sleepy eyes fly open with surprise as he says good night and turns abruptly away. Marguerite still feels the kiss as she watches him walk back toward the gathering at the fire. She knows it is a declaration that he is more than the polite suitor her family approves. He has left an imprint with his stolen kiss. She cannot erase it, but she does not love him.

She clasps her right hand over the silver bracelet on her arm as she continues through the avenue toward home.

. . .

Several weeks go by, and still Arosen doesn't appear. Marguerite is aware of Kenniontie and Atironta wondering and watching for her response to his absence, and she tries to go on as if it doesn't worry her, but she wonders herself. She has avoided Rowahokon around the village. Various groups are heading off for short stays at the hunting camps before the final harvest, and Gaianniana urges her again to come along with the group she and Desawennawen are leading.

"It will do you no good to stay and wait. It is only a few days, and he can find us if he comes before we're back."

"You're right. I'll come. I worry about Arosen, but it is a long trip and I'm sure he has business to take care of on the way." But she can't help wondering what has happened.

When the group comes together it includes Ohnwatsihon and several others, including Rowahokon.

"He only told us last night," Gaianniana looks apologetic.

Marguerite gives no answer but a droll, sideways look.

"He is kin to us," Gaianniana continues defensively. "I know you are waiting for François Arosen to return. Rowahokon knows it too."

Gaianniana's response only deepens her irritation. She has nothing to say. A year ago they would have burst out laughing at the weakness of Gaianniana's explanation. Now they walk on silently. The leaves are already dry and rustle on their branches as if the autumn were far advanced, though it is only the beginning of

Freshness Moon, a whole month before harvest time. The prolonged drought seems to be making the earth an old woman before her time.

The hunting party arrives at the mountain camp at dusk and makes camp hastily before darkness falls. When Marguerite rises the next morning, the sun is low and filters through the trees, setting patches of browning underbrush ablaze with a color like crushed rose hips. Despite her dismay at Rowahokon's presence and the nagging worry that Arosen will not return, she is eager to spend the day on a nearby pond with Gaianniana and Ohnwatsihon. There is nothing to do at Kahnawake now but wait, or so it feels to her—wait for Arosen, wait for the late corn and squash to ripen in the dry ground. She must also wait for another emissary from the English. Following the excitement of the Green Corn Festival, Achiendase and Kenniontie informed her that rekindled talks between the English and the French might bring another visitor with the turning of the leaves in the Freshness Moon. She is free to choose whether she will meet with anyone but, unless the visitor turns out to be someone she has reason to refuse, she knows what is expected of her when there are efforts at making peace.

Ohnwatsihon is kicking dirt at her heels. The dry earth plumes up around her. She is thinking of last night's dream. How many times has she dreamed it? In it, she is always a young man hunting with a rifle. She sees herself with her chestnut hair pulled back in a loose tail behind her head. She kneels in a thicket at dawn, dressed in dark buckskin, elbow propped on a raised knee, waiting for a herd of deer to trail down to a sparkling lake to drink. Instead she sees a man who signals to her, but she cannot understand him and she is filled with sorrow. He is neither a deer nor a man, and she neither shoots nor speaks to him. She has kept the dream a secret, making it much more important that she find some way to satisfy it, for a dream is always asking the dreamer for something. Its power can hurt her if she does not pay attention.

The big pond shimmers through the birches. Seeing the pond lifts her spirits, but there is a cruel edge. Its bright surface is little help when the rain has been kept from them for so long. A stunted harvest and a long winter lie ahead. Already she has seen ears of corn with rows of kernels gnarled and twisted as if cursed by witchcraft. Gazing up from the rocky path at the pale gauze of the sky, she sees a translucent crescent moon just above the crazy top of a far-off tamarack tree. It is like a ghost of the moon, the rim of a fingernail and also like the scar on the chin of the Dutchman she met with Atironta so long ago, the man who told her that the Williams family had returned to Deerfield. She remembers looking at his chin with its little scar in order to avoid his eyes. Now the new moon in the pale sky recalls his face, crooked, as if two spirits fought to rule it.

Gaianniana is waving from the rocks at the edge of the pond, and Tsihon is already at the water drinking.

They join Gaianniana, dropping their empty baskets beneath a hemlock tree, taking off their moccasins, and bathing their faces. The ground is like powder, with a scatter of tiny red-brown needles covering it. The water is black and silky. They don't linger on the shore. They have too much to do. Ohnwatsihon swims, while Marguerite and Gaianniana wade among the floating islands of lily pads, searching with their toes for lily roots, a crisp, delicious food. The water lilies are thick around them. The water is not very cold, though occasionally they feel the icy current of an underground spring. They speak little as they work, filling sacks with roots that they will scrape and slice for drying when they return to camp. Finally, they set their full baskets down on the shore so they can swim out beyond the shallows. Turning onto her back to watch the sky, Marguerite lets go of her worries. Arosen will come soon—before the visitor from Guerrefille, she tells herself.

. . .

When they return to camp they build only a small fire, careful to find flat rocks to line the pit so that the fire will not spread by underground roots. Desawennawen and Rowahokon have returned to camp with a doe, several rabbits, and a string of grouse. Others trail in behind them. They thank the doe. The drought has driven the game lower in the mountains this year. Perhaps it will make up for a meager harvest. Marguerite is sure that there will be bears around the camp, but they will not dare approach because of the dogs. She tosses a tidbit to Tsihon, who catches it expertly and settles down beside her.

. . .

A light rain begins toward morning. She smells the change even before she is roused from a dream she can't remember. She gets up herself and is glad to see that she is the first awake, though Gaianniana is stirring. She will be ready to help her stretch a skin over the rack where they have hung the venison to dry, giving thanks to it as a provider that sustains them.

"I saw the ring around the moon last night. It was so faint and it has been so long since we've had rain that I didn't think to cover things."

Gaianniana smiles. "Maybe if we had covered our food, the rain would have drifted past us. As it is, it isn't much yet."

She studies Gaianniana, wondering whether to speak to her about Rowahokon's kiss after the Green Corn Festival, but thinks better of it. A year ago there would have been no doubt. Their quick tongues would have turned the incident over like a pebble in a babbling brook, until it had been examined from every angle, polished, smoothed, stored in their common memory. Now, with a mental shrug, she decides that it is not worth discussing. After all, he has not tried again.

When they reach the inlet this morning, the warm rain is falling in large, soft drops, turning the dark, glassy water into a sea of widening circles, expanding until they catch the edge of the next and disappear. The water looks less inviting than it did yesterday. Mostly her thoughts are with Arosen. Is he on his way to her? Alive? Has he changed his mind? Traveling might be safer because of new negotiations between the English and the French. All are tired of the war. But the English may still be paying a bounty on enemy scalps, one that some men would kill to claim.

There are always those who thirst for blood, even among Christians. Samuel Williams has dispelled any doubt she may have had about that.

CHAPTER 23

When Marguerite arrives at early Mass after returning from the hunting camp, Arosen is standing on the men's side of the chapel. It is as if some fine strand of awareness draws her gaze. He makes a small sign with one hand to let her know that he has been watching for her. She closes her eyes for a moment and bright points of light stream behind them. It is impossible to keep her mind on the Mass. Achiendase's singsong voice seems to go on forever, the Canienga language flowing musically, her own voice merging with the others in each response. She listens for Arosen's as she sings, tries to catch sight of him again as she files up the aisle to take communion.

In front of the chapel, they greet each other formally under Kenniontie's gaze, except that they look straight into each other's eyes. Rowahokon passes by, heading for the path that skirts the woods to the west. To the east the sun has barely cleared the horizon and shines red behind a bank of clouds, tingeing the rapids. Kenniontie's greeting is reserved, and she throws Arosen a warning look as she parts from them. They take the path that leads directly through the woods. As they step into the woods, Marguerite slides her silver bracelet from beneath her sleeve to show him.

"This came to me on the day that I danced." Her eyes do not leave him for a moment, as if he might be gone if they didn't hold him. "It made me very happy, not only because it is so beautiful, but because I knew you were thinking of me," she says.

"I'm glad it reached you. The man who traded it to me said it came from very far west. It was traded along a very long chain. So he said."

"I believe it. I have seen nothing like it, not ever. I haven't taken it off since the day I danced. I think I won't ever take it off." She smiles up at him.

"I would have liked to be there to give it to you, but I thought it better not to come. I had a good reason."

"I worried when you didn't come sooner."

"I have done easier things than to stay away." There is a pause, and he suddenly looks worried. "You are glad that I'm here, aren't you, Marguerite Gannestenawi? A'onote? Nothing has changed?"

"No, François Arosen," she answers, smiling as she echoes him, using his formal name. "Nothing has changed."

They turn onto a narrower trail that cuts away from the main one. Arosen ushers her ahead of him. When they have gone a few yards he slips his hand around her waist and swings her to him, embracing her tightly before letting go.

"Let's go to the cedars," she says. "I want to know all about your time at the Western Door. I wondered about it every day you were there."

"Your mother gave me a forbidding look as we walked away just now," says Arosen. Marguerite looks up into the treetops. A flock of cedar waxwings flits from branch to branch. She isn't sure what to say to this, since she has avoided the subject with her family, hoping that Achiendase would speak to them and smooth the way now that she is baptized. As they step into the circle of cedars and seat themselves on the dry moss, Arosen takes her hand. "All the time I was away, not just recently but before, I have been working among the Haudenosaunee chiefs on ways to keep the peace among us in spite of Queen Anne's War and our different interests. Just days after you danced, I was given the title of Pine Tree Chief, the title my father earned in his healthy days, the one I told you I wanted to earn."

"Arosen, you must be very proud," she says almost shyly. "I thought that was a far-off dream."

"Sometimes, I think, it's better to work at something than to talk too much about it."

"I wanted to wait until you were here to talk to my parents about you. And now you have arrived with this good news." She looks down at her fancy tunic. "When I first came to Kahnawake my mother had sewn me a beautiful tunic with the tree of the Great Peace all in beads at its center. It will mean a great deal to her that you have earned the title of Pine Tree Chief." She looks at him. "I am a woman and a communicant now, and I am preparing to learn the medicine of the Otter Society. I can choose whom I marry, but I think my family will accept you gladly." They continue discussing their plans for the future.

"Look!" says Marguerite at last. "The sun was still red behind the clouds when we came here. Now it is high and white." She laughs. "You know, when I first came here with Gaia and Ohnwatsi-hon, we were almost found by a group of Dutchmen. We were terrified and I thought they had killed Tsihon. If I had known their language I would have gone with them. . . ."

"Do you ever wish you had gone?"

"No. It would be a different life if I had gone. Look at us here," she says, gesturing toward him. "How could I wish it were different?"

. . .

It is midday when Marguerite returns to the longhouse. Kenniontie is sitting outside weaving baskets. The loud buzz of cicadas in the trees makes the air around the house seem even hotter and drier.

"We won't need as many baskets this year. The corn is already whispering. It says, *I hope the hunting is good!*" says Kenniontie, looking up from her work.

"It says, *You better store up some good stories!*"

Marguerite laughs as she watches Kenniontie's deft fingers weave new staves into a broken basket. They have been preparing storage for the harvest for weeks now. Basketry, wood, and skin containers lie all around the rock in the sunny clearing in front of the house. They have had lean winters before and are not unduly concerned. There has always been fat within the lean.

Marguerite studies her mother's face as she joins her. Kenniontie looks up.

"Careful, those basket staves will hurt if you jab yourself," Kenniontie observes mildly. And then adds more seriously, "It will happen as you wish. I can see how it is with you and Arosen. Achiendase has spoken to us about you too. We were pleased to hear that Arosen has become a Pine Tree Chief, and he has shown his devotion to you. We will accept the marriage bread."

"I'm so happy to have your blessing." Marguerite throws her arms around her mother.

"There is more that I want to say. I know that you have wanted this, and I am happy for you," says Kenniontie. "But I wonder if you could wait a little before marrying, now that you know you have our blessing. Take your time and enjoy looking ahead."

Marguerite frowns. "Do you still think I'm not sure?"

"No, only that you are hurried by other worries. I know these visits from the English messengers worry you, and sometimes I think you fear they could take you away. They cannot make you go, married or not, Marguerite." Kenniontie has returned to her work, treating each strand as a thought as she weaves it into the basket she repairs. "It wouldn't hurt to wait."

"I have waited. I have waited a very long time."

Kenniontie smiles. "You know nothing of long," she answers.

"No. You are wrong about that. I waited for my English father. That was long," Marguerite replies firmly, then sees the hurt look on Kenniontie's face. "Not because I wanted to go back. But he took my brothers and my sister, and left me behind. I wanted to know that he did not *choose* to leave me. That was the important thing—not that I went back, only that he cared enough to come for me himself. You and Atironta would have come for me. I am certain of that. So, I know what is long. It is hard to explain, but the time that I have waited for Arosen has been longer because of what I know. I waited before, and my father never came. Now it is too late. Love can wither away." Marguerite looks at the drooping trees surrounding them, notices the buzz of cicadas again. Why can't Kenniontie give her consent simply? She withdraws her approval as she gives it. It is wearying and upsetting. It robs her of joy.

Kenniontie covers Marguerite's busy hand with her own. "You can walk into the river instead of diving. I know Achiendase is glad to let you marry soon, and Atironta and I are glad that you will marry in the chapel with a Mass. But the priests know nothing of these things. They do not marry, and, beyond that, these Europeans, even Achiendase, see everything as one way or another. It does not change for them with circumstance. They wear heavy clothes because the Cold Moon has come, not because it is cold."

"It is not because of Achiendase that we want to marry in the church. My own voice grows stronger all the time. It gathers strength from my new names but has always been my own and guided me. This is the right thing for me to do. I am glad that you will stand by us." She looks into Kenniontie's eyes. "We will be married as soon as a wedding can be prepared. Gaianniana's mother will bring the marriage bread to Asientie."

"A'onote Marguerite Gannestenawi," says her mother. "I hear the voice that guides you, and I believe it. I've never said it, but I have feared losing you, one way or another. I see now that I will not. All your names belong to you, and you do speak with one voice. I will speak with one voice too in blessing you."

Marguerite sighs with relief. Her first business, now that she has spoken to Kenniontie, is to find Arosen. The sun is well past its noontime height. The world is dusty, trees and shrubs thirsting in the midday sun. She feels that her step on the dry earth will make grasses grow in her wake, that a glance at the drooping trees will make their sap flow as her blood does. How could it be otherwise? She is a woman, blessed and blessing, graced and gracing; she is powerful; she has attained her seat and can proceed from there to make a life. If her feet do not immediately cause springs to flow where she steps, they will, they will. It is in her power; she has always known it.

The village rests at midday. A few women still go about their business, but mostly people sit in the shade, or, if their houses are cooler, inside them. Such mystery in houses, she thinks—some cool, some not, and who knows why? For sometimes they seem to have equally favorable sites to catch a breeze, equally thick roofs to repel the heat or seal out cold. Yet one is cool in summer and welcoming in winter, and the other is not. There must be something of the builder in every house. Marguerite knows how her house will be when it comes time to build one. It is in her blood now, that knowledge.

Now she is nearing Gaianniana's family's house. Arosen is likely to be there with Gaianniana's father and possibly her own, but he won't know anything. Atironta wouldn't tell him. It's women's business. She sees in her mind the three men sitting there, and Gaianniana and her husband and mother might be there too. Her step slows because there is only one whom she wants to see at the moment.

An evening grosbeak flutters from a thicket and lights in the branches of a plum tree ahead. Marguerite slows down. Dressed for a wedding in his bold yellow, she thinks, but late in the season for him to be here. Take your mate and fly away; go quickly; don't let the crazy weather fool you! A bird out of season is a messenger. She comes to a halt a few feet from the bird's perch. She fixes her eyes on the yellow bird as he shifts his feet and bills the branch. A breeze comes up and raises goose bumps on her arm. The bird looks at her from under his stern, yellow brow. She closes her eyes but continues to see him. He takes off in a swift, dipping flight away from the path toward where the stream trickles, thirsty and meek where it had run smooth and bracing. She follows the messenger to see where he will lead her.

Light streams through the woods around her. Brilliant red

bunchberry gleams from beneath leaves untouched by drought. Lichen splotches rocks in green—pale and glowing. The bird waits and takes off again in its loopy flight, still heading toward the shriveling stream. Wait! Some small part of her mind resists. But her feet keep carrying her farther into the orchard that spills toward the stream. The bird lights and flies, tilting its cockaded head to watch for her each time. It leads her down to where the stream is as full as in springtime. She turns to look behind her, and the orchard is in flower. The moss beneath her feet is springy and fragrant, and two otters sway down to the water where a little pool has formed. One glides and rolls in the pool. The orchard is alive with birdsong.

The otter that remains on the shore stands to regard her. Her eyes are deep and Marguerite looks into them transfixed. She sees her red-haired mother there, Kenniontie, and Asientie. The otter does not speak or sing this time as she did by the stream, when Marguerite first saw her in the snow. The orchard seems to drop its petals and turn green then brown, then etch the sky while the stream freezes, runs, dries up, and flows again.

Suddenly, there is a child in a tight bodice with long, wide sleeves sitting next to her, sewing unfamiliar symbols in brightly colored threads onto a white cloth held taut in a ring. The child looks at her as if she knows something Marguerite does not. She speaks in a faintly familiar language, which she understands without knowing any of the words. A man's voice, calling in the same language, is unintelligible. She turns toward it to try to hear it better, but the words have no sense for her. She turns back to look at the girl and she sees instead the girl's spirit, a bright light, enter the otter. She looks at the otter again and sees four small ones behind it. It looks back at her and leads its little legion away.

"A'onote! Marguerite Gannestenawi!"

The noon sun glares white through the drooping leaves. Marguerite looks around her; she is still on the path to Gaianniana's house. She lifts her hand to her brow and narrows her eyes. François Arosen is walking toward her, his moccasins raising plumes of pale dust: he is beautiful. Marguerite shakes off her enchantment and runs to him as if it has been eons since she has seen him.

"What is the matter?" he asks as his arms enfold her.

"Nothing. We must look for Achiendase and ask Gaiannana's mother to bring the marriage bread to Asientie. We can be married as soon as Achiendase can prepare a Mass!" She looks up; her eyes alight. "I was looking for you."

Arosen swings her away from him. "You didn't look as if you were looking for anyone," he retorts with a grin. "Waiting, perhaps. I was looking for you."

"Did you know?"

"Nobody told me, but I knew."

Marguerite shakes her head lightly as if to clear it. There is nothing to say yet of the bird and the otter, the voice and her young self.

CHAPTER 24

"Marguerite Gannestenawi!" It is Marie Gentiyo calling out to her as she approaches the longhouse with Gaianniana. "A beautiful day for a wedding!"

There are storm clouds gathering to the west, but so far the rain has held off. Asientie and Gaianniana's mother exchanged the wedding bread in the old way two weeks ago, sealing the traditional agreement between families that their children will marry, and the marriage date was formally announced. Marguerite and Arosen have worked separately for the past two weeks—she decorating her fancy dress with new ribbons and beadwork and making containers and other small items they will need for their new house, he building a small house for them on land across the orchard from Asientie's. Marguerite has tried to push the thought of the visitor from her mind, but it nags at her. His coming now would spoil her wedding. The men of their families have built an arbor leading to the chapel, a frame of silvered saplings decorated with corn, bright blue flax, black-eyed Susan, and other hardy meadow flowers. Atironta is working on something at Gaianniana's family's house, but no one will tell what it is.

"I hope the rain holds off a little longer. It's too late to do much for us now that we're ready to harvest," says Gaianniana. "Are you happy? You look so beautiful."

"I'm happy. I'm glad you're here. It's strange, but I feel nervous too," says A'onote.

Marie Gentiyo and Gaianniana exchange a look, and Marie laughs happily. "Of course you are. Your life is changing, A'onote Marguerite Gannestenawi. I was nervous on my wedding day too."

"When did you last see Arosen?" asks Gaianniana.

"We agreed last night that we wouldn't meet until we see each other at the chapel."

"And what do you think?" asks Marie. "He's disappeared?"

"He suddenly seems almost like a stranger to me, as if he'll be a different person when I see him."

"Well," Marie Gentiyo looks more serious now, "in a way, he will be. And so will you. Don't you think so, Gaia?"

Marguerite looks at them questioningly.

"It's true." Gaianniana looks thoughtful. "I never thought of it that way, but it is. You are both different—together, even though you are not the same person. It's hard to explain. You know that you are joined and that you know each other, but when the ceremony ends, it has changed you both. You have to look again to recognize him, the way you have to look at someone who has earned a new name, because there is something new in that person."

Marie laughs. "How serious we are! Now, let's paint your cheeks and finish dressing your hair. We've brought some pretty feathers for you," says Gaianniana. "Kenniontie is coming in a few minutes to go to the chapel with us. My father is so proud to be giving you away!" Although the ceremony is to be conducted by Achiendase in the chapel, some aspects of it will follow traditional Canienga patterns, like giving the ceremonial role to Onwekowa instead of to Atironta.

"Our families will be woven tight on all sides now, since your mother brought the marriage bread for Arosen's family, your father is giving me away, and Marie Gentiyo is married to our younger uncle." Marguerite takes both her friends' hands. "We are truly three sisters."

They turn to see Kenniontie walking toward them, tall and elegant in a quilled dress of rose and blue. Marguerite runs to embrace her and is glad to see that her mother looks almost as happy as if she were the one getting married. Kenniontie places a beaded stole around her shoulders. After Gaianniana fastens one more feather in Marguerite's hair, they set off for the Kahnawake chapel.

It is late afternoon as they approach the arbor leading into the church. A chorus of flutes and water drums, gourds and turtle shell rattles greet her. The chanting has already begun. Her uncle takes her arm to lead her through the arbor and into the chapel, where Arosen waits. There is some distant thunder, but the sky doesn't open until they have entered the chapel, where Marguerite hardly remembers going down the aisle past the standing congregation, Arosen stepping out of the wings to meet her.

Achiendase, his usual black robe brightened by a beaded chasuble, looks from one to the other and begins. Thunder and the drumming of rain on the chapel roof drown out some of his words, but she hears him ask her if she will take this man in sickness and health, for richer or poorer, and she hears her own voice ring out strongly, and soon she and her husband are heading up the aisle toward the open door. By the time they reach it, the rain has stopped and the sun is setting on a drenched world. There is a feast and dancing at the central longhouse and only a few more showers during the night.

Waking the next morning in her own house, Marguerite finds herself laughing in amazement at the gifts people left, slipping in during the feasting and dancing. She and Arosen had seen nothing when they returned to the dark house the night before.

"Arosen, look!" she exclaims as her eyes fall on a chest carved in the style of the chest where Asientie keeps her medicine bundles and other things of special value to her. "Look what my father has been working on all this time!" Inside the chest she finds an assortment of quilled baskets and carved gourd containers, an iron pot from Montreal, household items Kenniontie has made and traded for. Tucked into a corner of the chest, she notices something small, wrapped carefully in soft doeskin and tied with a beaded ribbon. She unties it carefully and finds her silver cup, no longer blackened but shining as it did when it was given to her, a frightened little girl, by her red-haired mother, as she told her that, whatever happened, she would go with her always.

Eunice A'onote Marguerite Gannestenawi Williams looks at her husband, eyes suddenly brimming. "I haven't looked at this cup in a very long time," she says. "We are truly blessed. I will tell you about it."

• • •

The next day they leave for a camp by a brook that Arosen has told her about. When they arrive in the high mountains that make up part of the Canienga hunting grounds, they build a lean-to on a smooth shelf at the top of a waterfall. A full moon, golden as a squash blossom, rests heavy on the horizon. Here the mountain storms have kept the rivers higher. It is growing cold, but they can swim and fish before Marguerite returns to help her family with the late harvest and hunting season begins in earnest. Next spring, not only will she have her house and the fields of her family and friends to tend but she will tend her own fields too.

When she hears Tsihon barking on the third morning, Marguerite pulls herself shivering from the pool at the bottom of the falls, feeling the approach of winter even in the sun. She wrings her wet hair, thinking Arosen is coming down from the camp, and quickly pulls her tunic over her head when she sees that it is Ohnwatsihon approaching with another dog trotting by his side. Amazed that he has come so far, Marguerite calls out to him when he is close enough to hear her over the rushing brook.

"Come and swim! The water's freezing, but the rocks are already warm!"

He is stepping out of the woods onto the smooth, stony shelf when she notices the intensity of his expression. His eyes remain on the dog as he greets her. Marguerite sets her hand on his shoulder to put him at ease.

"I'm glad to see you, cousin."

The boy looks at her now with a round-eyed look of surprise that reminds her of the first time she saw him, a toddler in Sientiesie's arms, afternoon light drifting like dust through the smoke hole. Now he has twelve winters, almost a man.

"What is it?" she asks.

"The Reverend Williams, your English father, has come to see you," he answers.

Marguerite feels only a kind of stupor. "My English father," she repeats in shock. "No one said it would be him. Is he at the mission or only on his way?" Anger surges up in her. How could her come to Kahnawake now? It seems wrong, when she has come so far in her own life, has earned her name and all the respect that goes with it, has been baptized and married, and is happy when she looks to the future. His coming feels like a threat to all she has achieved, but she notices her heart is racing, and she isn't sure why.

"He is in Montreal. They hope you will come home."

"I'll come, but I must get Arosen and pack up first."

Ohnwatsihon nods again. Uncertainly, it seems to Marguerite.

"We won't be very long. Don't worry. You will eat and rest before going back. He has waited many years to come and gave no warning. It won't make any difference if you rest while we get ready. So. You have become a runner! This is a long way for your first big errand."

When they start up to their little camp at the top of the waterfall, they meet Arosen making his way down to the pool.

"I was just coming to find you," she says. "Ohnwatsihon has brought surprising news."

"So the Reverend has come. Is he at the mission or in Montreal?" Arosen seems to take the news in stride, though he couldn't have known, and his steadiness feels reassuring.

"He is in Montreal. He might want to rest a few days after coming through the mountains. It is a long way."

"I think your Reverend is more likely to have traveled by ship from Boston and will be in a hurry to see you. He will be waiting for you at the mission. I am sure of it."

"*My* Reverend!" She looks closely at Arosen to see if he means to be cruel. "He gave no warning." She shakes her head.

"Perhaps he didn't want you to have time to think about it. He didn't expect you would be away so near harvest time. Do you want to see him?"

"I don't know. It seems to me I must." She sits down suddenly, feeling her knees might give way.

Arriving back at the camp, they look around, knowing they will not be able to return until next year. But the idyll is over. As they pack up, she thinks that they could go somewhere else and avoid this meeting, but that would only be postponing it. She folds a deerskin into a basket pack. They stop only briefly at the foot of the falls so Arosen can swim.

Farther from the falls the stream gets very shallow. Even the mountain thunderstorms haven't created bounty here. They have more than a day's trek ahead of them, but once they come down from the high peaks, the way is flat. As they get closer on the second day, Marguerite begins to fall back and notices Arosen occasionally looking behind him. He wants to be sure she is still with him, she thinks. They have withdrawn into their thoughts, descended into a silence different from the easy quiet that has bound them together during the past few days. They are sealed within themselves, less sure of each other. Arosen would not have needed to look behind him yesterday.

A knot forms in Marguerite's throat. Images of her English father flit like the shadows of trees or passing clouds. One moment he is fixed in her mind and the next he is gone. She sees him reading scripture by the fire, but only as a dim shape that doesn't come clear. She imagines him pinching the bridge of his nose, a gesture that brings another flood of images. She quickens her pace to outdistance them and calls out to Arosen.

"Arosen! Walk with me. We are almost there. I am afraid."

"You must be afraid that you will leave me then."

"No! Not of that." She puts her arm around his waist but feels disembodied. She *is* afraid. What can she be afraid of? She feels that if she looks at the Reverend, like the kidnapped brides in stories, taken from the world of sun to the world of ice or from the earthly world to the sky world, she will never be at home again in any place. Ahead, where the path empties into the meadow surrounding the mission, she sees Kenniontie and Atironta waiting. Ohnwatsihon had run ahead this morning to let them know she was nearly there.

Achiendase comes outside to greet them, and it is all as it was so many years ago, except that Arosen is at her side. Achiendase ushers Marguerite and Arosen into the empty hall, while Kenniontie and Atironta wait outside. She agrees to sit on a chair opposite the one set out for the Reverend while the others stand, a concession that she suddenly regrets. But she must abide by it. Arosen is stationed behind her, where she cannot see him. She hooks her arm over the back of the chair, but that is uncomfortable. She pulls her legs underneath the chair, crossing her ankles and leaning back, her hands cradled in her lap. She doesn't want her discomfort to show. More elaborate clothes might have made her feel stronger. She looks down at her bracelet, and as she lifts her head there are men coming into the room. She feels Arosen's steady hand on her shoulder. She tilts her chin toward the ceiling, but she sees the Reverend coming into the room anyway. Even though he approaches with several other men, she is sure she has picked him out. He separates himself from the others and seats himself across from her. Still, she doesn't look straight at him.

Achiendase's voice seems to admonish her. "Marguerite. This is the Reverend Williams."

"Eunice!" The room is silent except for the name. "Eunice." Some indistinguishable English words follow.

"Marguerite! Will you greet your father?" asks Achiendase.

She has told herself that she will not look at him. Now she is surprised that she cannot look at him or speak, even in her own tongue.

Achiendase waits before continuing. "Your father will speak, and we will translate for him." He nods at a Dutchman she has met before, and she lets her eyes slide over him, the scar-chin, whose name she does not want to know.

Her English father keeps his eyes on her when he speaks. It is hard not to look when she can feel them on her. She wants to verify the color, so vivid to her, but those eyes might do her harm. He believes he is a saint, she tells herself, and I am not. That is what would be in his eyes. She reminds herself of what a real saint is, what Achiendase, who would never claim to be a saint, has taught her about what it means to be one. If she looks at him she might forget. She saw enough when he walked into the room. He is tall, but slighter than she remembered. He has hair the color of a deer hide, like the man who turned into a deer in her dream. She closes her eyes to deflect the intensity of his focus. When she opens them again, she can feel that her English father is looking straight at her. His gaze pulls like a wave, drawing sand from beneath her feet. She wants to plant herself more firmly on the ground instead of perching birdlike on the mission-house chair. She thinks of the yellow grosbeak, the deep eyes of the otter, the child's quick spirit flitting into the otter like lightning. She thinks of her husband. If she can get through this without looking at the Reverend, she will be safe.

"The Reverend Williams says that your brothers and sister long to see you. Stephen is grown and at college, and Esther is a young woman." This is just what the Dutchman told her all those years ago.

She looks blankly at the planked floor. The names evoke a

landscape as distant as infancy, as attractive as a fairy tale, an ingenious snare set to attract her. She sees this man, her father, embracing her in the snow before sending her off with Atironta, but
as if it were a story told about someone else.

"You have two half-brothers whom you have not seen and who
long to know you, and a stepmother who will welcome you with all
her heart." Again, these words have no power to move her. She
remembers the first time she heard them. Achiendase pauses and
looks at her. "Marguerite. Would it hurt you to give this man a
word? It is uncharitable to withhold even that."

In the silence Marguerite feels the Reverend's hunger. She wishes
she could turn to look at Arosen. His steadying hand is enough,
she tells herself. She distracts herself by watching small changes in
Achiendase's expression. Foreign words percolate through her.
Some she understands, but they float free of context. The Dutchman speaks French and even her own tongue, but Achiendase continues to translate. The words work on her like water boring a
kettle-hole into stone, a slow and steady torture. More than anything, they make her angry. She lets the halting English and the
rise and fall of the more-familiar French recede.

At last the men no longer address themselves to her, but stand
aside speaking to one another. Finally, she hears Arosen speak up.
"She has told me it would be easier, if you had not married so soon,"
he tells the Reverend. Arosen has found a way to end this torture.

She looks at the floor as the Reverend Williams approaches,
feels his hand's weight on her head. She wants to close her eyes but
stays focused on a knot in the plank next to her chair.

"Daughter." The hand rests for a moment at the nape of her neck.

"He knows you will not go with him, A'onote," says Arosen.

"But he has asked that you consider making a visit in the spring. I would go with you. You would not have to stay there longer than you wished."

She stands and takes Arosen's hand. "*Jagoghte*," she replies. Maybe not. She has come so far. For now, one world is enough for her.

AUTHOR'S NOTE

THE MOURNING WARS is a work of fiction. However, Eunice Williams and most of her family really were kidnapped in a raid on Deerfield, Massachusetts, on February 29, 1704, when Eunice was seven years old. The surviving members of the family were taken to Canada or the Green Mountains of Vermont, where they and many of their neighbors were dispersed among various French and Indian groups. The raid on Deerfield was one of the earliest and most notorious in Queen Anne's War, a conflict between the English and the French that had spread to the colonies from Europe, where it was called the War for the Spanish Succession. In addition to Eunice and her English family, many of the other characters in *The Mourning Wars* are based on historical figures. These include Joanna Kellogg, Governor Vaudreuil, François Arosen, and Zebediah Carter (whose real name was Zebediah Williams, though he was apparently no relation to Eunice's family), among others.

I have used known incidents and practices as springboards for invention, and I have, in one case, changed the date of an event for the purpose of narrative structure. The Reverend John Williams's second visit to Kahnawake occurred two years later than I have it in the story. It seemed to me that the psychological truth of Eunice's response to him would have been the same.

Several generations of Williams men, all prominent New England ministers, and others who knew the Williams family have recounted parts of Eunice's story in their sermons, letters, histories, and diaries. As the most famous captive from Deerfield, the Reverend Williams was greeted with great fanfare upon his return to New England and, because Eunice was his daughter, her fate was of greater interest than the fates of other captives who remained in Canada with the Indians or French. Her father described his own captivity and that of his children and neighbors in *The Redeemed Captive Returning to Zion*, based on a sermon he gave in Boston upon his return. His account was published in several editions during the eighteenth and nineteenth centuries. More recently, historian John Demos explored the impact of the raid through several generations. But Eunice's experience remains largely a mystery with no record in her voice, except a single surviving letter to her brother Stephen, scribed for her many years after this story takes place.

I have tried to be as true as possible both to history and to the ancient culture of the people known to the French and English settlers as the Maqua, or the Mohawk. Documents from the period refer more often to the Maqua, and I have chosen to have the people of Deerfield use this term. The people themselves, however, called themselves the Canienga. They belonged to the Haudenosaunee League, an alliance of five Iroquois nations, the Mohawk, Seneca, Oneida, Cayuga, and Onandaga. These nations were later joined by a sixth, the Tuscarora. During Queen Anne's

War, 1704 – 1713, native cultures were undergoing enormous trans-
formations caused by wars, disease, depletion of natural resources,
and the new religions and technologies brought to North America
by the Europeans.

My depictions of eighteenth-century Canienga ceremonies,
practices, and language can only be approximate. I have relied on
early reports in Allan Greer's *The Jesuit Relations* (New York: St.
Martin's Press, 2000), Horatio Hale's *The Iroquois Book of Rites*
(www.forgottenbooks.org, 2008), Dean Snow's *The Iroquois* (New
York: Wiley, 1995), and John Demos's *The Unredeemed Captive*
(New York: Knopf, 1995), which I picked up on my first visit to
Deerfield, among other accounts of Iroquois life and language. Most
of the Canienga words I use come from a glossary compiled by
Horatio Hale, a nineteenth century ethnographer, from Jesuit dictionaries by Bruyas and others and appended to an early edition of
Hale's *The Iroquois Book of Rites*. Later in the editorial process, I
also used more recent on-line dictionaries that became available. I
cannot vouch for the accuracy of any these renderings but hoped to
convey the sense of a complex and sophisticated living language.

Accounts by non-Native Americans are inherently limited. My
aim was a respectful rendering of how people might have lived at
this time and how one individual, Eunice Williams, might have
experienced her unique position as the most sought-after captive
and adoptee of her time.

I wanted to know how Eunice, as well as other captives, experienced and adapted to a society profoundly different from their
own, and I have tried to imagine this by reconstructing the world
Eunice entered as best I can. The Canienga of Kahnawake had left
their people in what is now New York State's Mohawk Valley. They
migrated to Canada in the mid-seventeenth century in order to

escape intense internecine warfare and religious persecution that had disrupted the Great Peace established by the five-hundred-year-old Haudenosaunee League. Many of the Canienga who migrated to Kahnawake adopted the Catholic faith of their French patrons, and most were closely allied with the French settlers and the Jesuit missionaries to New France. Although they remained part of the league, their alliance with the French divided them from most of the other Haudenosaunee, who had longstanding agreements with the English that they recorded in wampum belts.

Having family members captive in New France was especially disturbing to Puritans, like Reverend Williams, who believed that their conversion to Catholicism would likely result in their damnation. They considered Catholicism a dangerous heresy and therefore more insidious than Native American beliefs, which seemed merely ignorant to them.

Eunice Williams was inevitably caught up in political and religious tensions as she grew up. Nevertheless, she managed to take control of her life, ultimately embracing the culture of the Kahnawake people and the Catholic faith and marrying a Canienga man. While the Puritans prayed for their "poor relations held in Captivity," evidence shows that many, especially women and children, preferred their new lives. The choice to remain with their adoptive families must have been influenced by various factors, but I imagine that, in addition to being converted to Catholicism, they also came to appreciate a world where children were indulged and women were acknowledged to have power and allowed to play important roles in all realms of life.

As a child, Eunice probably would have found her adoptive parents' playful affection and the freedom they afforded her a welcome change from her Puritan upbringing. Puritan parents were admonished to show their love through vigilance and instruction. By all accounts, the Canienga held children in especially high esteem and tended to indulge them in ways that would have seemed impious to Puritans like Reverend Williams. They didn't share the Puritan belief that children were particularly vulnerable to sin and should be disciplined accordingly.

Unlike Eunice's mother, Haudenosaunee and other women of the eastern woodland tribes not only owned their houses and fields but also wielded considerable political power. According to laws laid down by the Haudenosaunee League, the elder women appointed chiefs and could remove them from office for poor leadership or wrongdoing. Decisions about going to war also had to be validated by the elder women, particularly in the case of Mourning Wars, by which they sought to replenish populations that had dwindled due to disease and warfare.

This book describes Eunice Williams's life only into early adulthood. However, the accounts of the New England Williams family and later histories tell us that Eunice Williams reestablished contact with her Deerfield family and visited them several times with her husband and children, although she never relearned English. When the French and Indian War made further visits impossible, Eunice and Stephen Williams corresponded for the rest of their long lives, albeit intermittently and through translators, a moving example of the power of early bonds overcoming a powerful cultural divide. The Kahnawake branch of the Williams family continued to visit their Massachusetts relatives for several generations. I believe Eunice would have been pleased by her descendents' efforts to embrace both worlds.

I am grateful to Simon Boughton, Katherine Jacobs, and Jodie Keller, who shepherded this book to publication with sensitivity and grace after its long life in a drawer, to Mark Siegel at First Second, who asked me to take the manuscript out of the drawer so he could read it, and to Neal Porter, who picked it up. Thanks too to my copyeditors and proofreaders, especially Manuela Kruger, for their patient and careful work with unfamiliar language and genealogies. I was moved by everyone's care to get things right. I would like to thank Kate and Jim Gorman for their encouragement upon reading early chapters, Maeve Kincaid Streep for so many bracing walks in all kinds of weather, and John Herman and his wife Ronnie for thoughtful and enthusiastic editorial and logistical advice while I worked on my MA at Manhattanville College. Finally, thanks to many poet friends and mentors and to my family near and far, who never failed to ask how it was going, even when it wasn't, and without whom nothing would happen.

SELECTED SOURCES

Demos, John. *The Unredeemed Captive*. New York: Knopf, 1994.

Hale, Horatio. *The Iroquois Book of Rites*, www.forgottenbooks.org.

Haudenosaunee: Kahnawake Branch of the Mohawk Nation.
www.kahnawakelonghouse.com.

Greer, Allan. *The Jesuit Relations: Travels and Explorations of the Jesuit Missionaries in New France*. New York: St. Martins, 2000.

Parkman, Francis. *A Half Century of Conflict, France and England in North America, Vol.II*. New York: Literary Classics of the United States, 1983.

Richter, Daniel K. *The Ordeal of the Longhouse*. Chapel Hill: University of North Carolina Press, 1992.

Russell, Howard S. *Indian New England Before the Mayflower*. Hanover, NH: University Press of New England, 1980.

Sheldon, George. *A History of Deerfield Massachusetts*. Greenfield: E.A. Hall & Co., 1895.

Smith, Mary P. Wells. *The Boy Captive of Deerfield*. Deerfield: Pocumtuck Valley Memorial Association, 1991.

Snow, Dean P. *The Iroquois*. Cambridge, MA: Blackwell Publishers, 1994.

Selected Sources

Wagner, Sally Roesch. *Sisters in Spirit*. Summertown, TN: Native Voices Book Publishing Company, 2001.

Williams, John. *The Redeemed Captive Returning to Zion*. Springfield: The H.R. Huntting Company, 1908.

ABOUT THE AUTHOR

Karen Steinmetz is a poet who lives in Nyack, New York, and teaches at Manhattanville College. *The Mourning Wars* is her first novel. Her poetry appears regularly in literary journals.